VASTLY UNDERRATED

Rachel Rafferty

'At This Point In My Life'

Tracy Chapman
(New Beginning)

Prologue

*I*f there had been some sort of sign, or if someone had warned me...I would have done things differently. How many times have I heard people say this? How many times have I said it to myself?

It was clear that I got distracted and allowed personal stuff to permeate professional matters. It was just this one time though, and I'd likely have forgotten it by now had the consequences not been so dire.

It seemed I couldn't be comforted by kind words of sympathy or communal support. Nothing worked, and I honestly believed the only solution available to me was to escape.

As a student of psychology, I looked to my books for advice. I got overwhelmed with too much information but the main message I gleaned was that shit happens. And when it does, we have to do our best to pick up the pieces, deal with it and move on.

Chapter One

As I heard the key turn in the front door, I felt a slight knot form in my tummy. Not a tight one, not firm, just a loose, haphazard one. What was that? Not excitement. I didn't feel lifted. Not disappointment either. The sound of the door opening didn't bring me down. It wasn't an extreme emotion, nothing I could put my finger on.

Maybe that lack of identification was indicative of my ten year relationship with John. Unemotional overall, but in no way threatening or divisive. We were comfortable in our middle age and didn't give much thought to our relationship's lack of direction. That said, I was thinking about it now.

'Hey Deb, I'm home. How goes it and what's for dinner?' he hollered from the hall.

Honestly, sometimes I felt like I was living with a teenager. He was fifty-two years old!

'I'll bake that quiche in a few minutes. I think it's out of date today. I'm just finishing up module three of...'

'You can't be too careful with eggs, Debra. Get that in the oven soon, it'll be no good tomorrow.'

He had no interest in my studies. 'Preheat the oven, John,' I shouted back from my snug seat at the living-room table. Everything was just as I liked it in here—my dimly-lit lamp to the right, the window behind me and my precious, patchwork armchair tucked into the corner. I'd often turn it to face the window and watch passersby in our bustling neighbourhood. That was my favourite spot in our house. I could sit there for hours and read, taking breaks to check out the view and see what my neighbours were up to.

Sometimes I'd just sit in silence and reflect upon my day, often with a knowing smile remembering a breakthrough I'd had with one of my students. John knew not to annoy me when I was in one of my trances like that. He'd pop his head in for a chat, but once he saw me in my armchair he'd head off on his own for a walk, or to the shops or whatnot.

'What temp...?'

'One-eighty,' I preempted.

It would take ten minutes for the oven to preheat. I looked over the last few bullet points in my document. While moving on from teacher to counsellor to therapist seemed like a natural progression, I still found the content of my new studies earth-shattering. I wished I'd known even a fraction of this stuff when I began working as a secondary-school teacher twenty-eight years ago. In hindsight, I should have done a psychology degree first, and then followed on with the counselling element. Anyway, *you live and learn,* as they say, and I'd have another fifteen years or so before retirement to benefit from this newfound knowledge.

I had no recollection of touching on themes such as adolescent identity and self-esteem analysis when I got my career-guidance counselling qualification from UCDN. It seemed perfunctory back then, nothing but researching college courses and career paths, while keeping on top of new educational developments. Of course, I still did that now, but I've found that I'd get completely immersed in the students' lives and it wasn't just about their future careers. It was about their current predicaments in school, like what subjects they were failing, what was happening at home, who was hungover and who just got dumped. They told me everything. Maybe they thought I was safe because they knew I wasn't a parent.

I heard the ding and got up to put the quiche in.

*   *   *

'A degree is more prestigious,' I said.

'I know, but wouldn't it be easier to get a job if I did the business diploma along with German? If I choose the arts degree, I can't do business as a second subject,' said Callum.

'What did you tell me your favourite subjects were?' I tried to get my sixth-year pupil to think less practically.

'Irish and German, but like, the only thing

I could do with them is teach and I don't want to be a teacher. I want to earn money, so I think an international language along with business or economics would be a good choice.' He made his point loud and clear.

'Well, first of all, teachers make money, you know. Look at me, I'm not exactly destitute and I'm in my third decade of teaching,' I winked, but I don't think he noticed my tiny eyes behind my glasses. 'Is this advice you're getting from your parents, Callum?'

'Well, they're not too fond of the idea of an arts degree, but I think it's because university fees cost a fortune. The business diplomas are way more affordable. And I could live at home and catch a bus to college.'

He had a point. He came from a down-to-earth family. But my training as a career-guidance counsellor was to encourage my students to follow their dreams and choose third-level courses according to their favourite subjects in secondary school. Nevertheless, financing one's dream was a huge issue and I couldn't very well go against his parents' wishes.

'That's true, Callum. I understand. How are your grades in business? I know languages are your strong point.'

'I get by. Mostly C pluses, but I got a B in economics last term.'

'That's good. Keep studying hard. You've made good choices on your third-level application form, very relevant to your interests and that's a great start. One of my past pupils did German and economics so I'll get some info from her about the course and share it with you. See you at this time next week, okay?' I smiled.

'Thanks, Ms Devlin,' he smiled back.

I wished all of my students were as forthcoming as Callum, but my next three career chats went more like—

'So, what course did you apply for?' And, the response—

'Dunno, Miss.'

'Well, what's your favourite subject?'

'Dunno' or, worse still—

'Don't like any of 'em.'

It took very excruciating dissections of their subjects to find something that they didn't hate and match it to one of the courses they'd applied for. At least that was a start and gave us something to work with. We still had time to make last minute changes on the application form, if necessary. Otherwise, I'd proceed to set targets for each student to give them a focus for their exam prep.

I stayed in school well after the home-time bell, as I usually did. I liked to get my to-do list completed before leaving and was affectionately known by my colleagues as a workaholic. They also availed of my counselling services, especially the younger members of staff who were thinking of taking up permanent positions or going on career breaks. Staying in late after school didn't feel like work to me, though. I was simply doing what I loved and was lucky enough to get paid for it.

I didn't have small children to rush home to, an elderly parent to mind or a yappy puppy to walk. I only had John. And he only had me. We had each other. And our comfortable house. And our jobs. He was happy in his professional life in the civil service and I found my job exhilarating enough to talk about right through dinner most evenings.

*   *   *

The next morning I got an email from Callum. He wanted to talk. I really didn't have time. My schedule was full, but he was such a lovely, polite student, one of my favourites in fact, so I gave him five minutes of what should have been my break time.

'What's up?' I asked, when he entered my office. It wasn't big enough to call a classroom. If I needed to speak to more than three students at once, I'd go and visit them in their base classroom. Space was scarce in Sacred Heart Secondary School in north County Dublin.

'Hi, Ms Devlin,' he said, looking more downcast than I'd ever seen him.

'Is everything okay, Callum? Did something happen?'

He was making me nervous. His eyes were

welling up.

'It's em, it's just...' He paused and coughed. I got up and poured him a glass of water from the jug on my desk. I was thinking maybe someone belonging to him had died, but then he'd hardly be in school if that was the case.

'It's Glenda, this girl I've been seeing.' He looked up, crestfallen.

I exhaled, relieved. It was only this, I thought. Young love and the heartache that went with it. He would get over this. He must have noticed the sense of relief on my face.

'What?' he asked. 'Do you know her or something?'

'Oh, no I don't, Callum. I'm just glad that nobody has died. I thought you were going to tell me something terrible.'

'But it is something terrible.' He looked at me with anguish in his eyes. Bless his little heart, I thought. There'd be plenty more girlfriends for him in whatever college he ended up in. I couldn't help a sympathetic smile.

'Are you laughing at me too?' he asked, accusingly.

'Callum! No! I'm sympathising. I'm sorry you broke up with your girlfriend and...'

'That's not what this is about.' He looked down and put his head in his hands.

'Then, what is it about? Because I have no idea.' I very quickly turned serious. He was in bits, crumbling a little more with each word he spoke.

'I met her at the disco last month. The one in the community centre, open to all, not just the local schools. That was where I met Glenda and we got on well. I got her number and we've been texting. We met twice since then and she made it clear she really likes me. She's been posting pictures of us together and saying I'm her new boyfriend.' He took a few breaths. I waited.

'One of my friends saw the photo of us together and...and she recognised Glenda. It's her little sister's friend from gymnastics.'

I began to realise where this was going now. 'Little? How much younger?' I asked, showing concern.

'She's fourteen,' he said and almost cried. He wiped his brow. 'Everyone found out and they're all calling me a paedo now. I didn't know! I swear, I didn't know! She told me she was eighteen, the same as me and in sixth year too. Turns out, she's only in second year.'

'Oh Callum, I believe you. You didn't know. With makeup and high heels, girls can make themselves look any age. It was a mistake. Don't beat yourself up about this...'

He looked up immediately. 'I'm not,' he said. 'But everyone else is.' And with that, he got up and walked out.

'Callum!' I called him. 'Callum, come back. We're not finished.'

But he was gone. Like a flash. Gone.

Chapter Two

'Jeez, what's going on?' I asked as I entered the school staffroom the next morning. I noticed heads down, which was unusual, and some were texting on their phones with panic-stricken faces. Normally on a Friday, everyone was in a good mood, as someone would bring cakes to celebrate the upcoming weekend.

'Don't tell me there's a whole school inspection?' I asked, quickly jumping to a conclusion. The inspectorate had been threatening our school with one for the past two years.

Maureen, the principal, got up and walked over to me. 'Debra,' she said. 'One of our pupils took his own life last night.'

Ashen—that was the colour my mother said I used to turn on hearing bad news. I was pale anyway and normal colour wouldn't return to my face for days. In this case, however, it was weeks.

'Who?' I asked. She held my shoulders.

'It was one of our sixth years,' she said.

I froze. My eyes darted from side to side as my mind filled with images of every single sixth-year pupil in our school. I knew them all. But for some reason, one image stuck. The somewhat unnerving encounter I'd had with Callum. I'd been planning to record it in my log. But what happened? Why didn't I? That wasn't like me at all. I always accomplished my to-do list. What knocked me off my path yesterday?

Then I remembered the phone call from my sister, Patricia. She finally went and got that lump checked. I'd been nagging her about it since she first mentioned it a few months ago. She'd fobbed me off each time. I had to ring the GP myself and make the appointment for her. I rang her husband, Christy, and told him to bring her to Doctor Khan on Macmillan Road at nine o'clock.

She phoned me in the afternoon to give me an update and that was when my to-do list went out the window. Patricia... I cursed my darling sister, who I loved dearly. I cursed her silently in my head for making me forget my follow-up notes yesterday.

Maureen made me sit down as news of the event trickled in from one source or another. Callum's mother had found him in the garden shed last night, a stool kicked away towards the door. She didn't know how long he'd been hanging there.

After extensive investigations, we established that I was the last person who saw him alive in school. The last person he spoke with. The last person he opened his tortured, teenage soul to. The last person to call his name.

And I'd just let him go.

*   *   *

It would be impossible to count the number of

times I retraced my steps that afternoon. One thing was for sure, and it would no doubt get added to my list of regrets—I didn't record what happened at our meeting. I had no written record of what Callum said or how he appeared. I had no follow-up arranged for him about his next step. I had no advice logged about how he should deal with the onslaught of derogatory names he'd been called. Or no recommendations about what he should do about the unjustified abuse he had endured in the twenty-four hours since the photo was released. I didn't even get the chance to let him know that I thought it WAS unjustified.

It hadn't been a planned meeting in the sense that he'd just sent an unexpected email that morning. Our scheduled meeting about his third-level subject choices wasn't due until the following week. Despite the shock and trauma darting through my brain, I could recall that it was during morning break that he came to see me. I gave him five minutes of my break, because I was so fond of him and it was unusual that he wanted to see me ahead of our scheduled slot.

I remembered being surprised when I saw how solemn he looked. There was no lightness in his eyes and he didn't smile at me like he usually did. I also remembered making light of what I thought was his heartache following a breakup. I shouldn't have done that. I shouldn't have shown a sense of relief on my face until I'd heard the full story.

He'd left my office in a flash. As I called after him, the caretaker was passing by and looked my way. I shook my head, shrugged and raised my eyes. I was thinking—*silly me, calling no one in an empty corridor!* The caretaker smiled and nodded in agreement, both of us minimising the emotions of teenagers who storm out of rooms.

I'd never forgive myself for that. I SHOOK MY HEAD, SHRUGGED AND RAISED MY EYES. I've had twenty-eight years of experience working with teenagers. I should have known better. I should have done more. I should have run after him, sent out a search party or called his parents to let them know of his distress.

But all I did was smile back at the caretaker and jot Callum's name on my to-do list as a reminder to log our meeting later. Then, I dashed to the staffroom for a cuppa before my next class.

The rest of the day was busy with one class after another. I didn't even get to the staffroom at big-break. The young history teacher, Katie, popped in to chat about her career-break plans to take off and teach for a year in Dubai. We lunched together in my room as I reassured her she was doing the right thing. She'd come home with huge savings and could put it towards her mortgage fund.

As soon as she left I had back-to-back meetings with sixth-year students, and it was only after my last one at half past three that I looked at my to-do list. That was when my phone rang.

I wouldn't normally answer until after the school bell at twenty to four, but it was Patricia and she'd had her appointment that morning about the suspicious lump under her right arm.

'Well?' I said on answering.

'Ah, Debra, it wasn't as straightforward as I'd hoped. He examined it and he didn't like it. He's sending me for a biopsy.'

'Oh, okay, so he couldn't diagnose it there and then?'

'No, and to tell the truth, I didn't like the look on his face. He was very muted too, he...he didn't say much.'

'Well, it's better he kept his opinions to himself. I mean how could he really know anything just by looking and prodding? I'm glad he's sending you to get properly checked out. When is the biopsy?'

'Tomorrow,' Patricia said.

'Tomorrow? So soon? How did you...?'

'Doctor Khan made the appointment for me and when he described the lumps, I got to jump the queue.'

'Lumps? Plural?' I was stunned. She only mentioned one lump to me, she never said there was more than one. Never!

'Yeah, Debra, I didn't want to worry you.'

'Patricia! Weren't YOU worried? Why did you delay going to the doctor?'

'I was scared so I put it out of my head. I took on a few extra shifts at the library to take my mind off it and…oh, I know I messed up. And now I'm terrified. I don't want to go to this biopsy, but Christy has me addled. He's upstairs now packing a bag for me.'

'A bag? Will you be there overnight?'

'Yeah, they said to bring an overnight bag. I think they're going to do an ultrasound too.'

'Oh,' I said, thinking that's a lot of tests in quick succession. I could hear the fear in her voice. Oh no, I thought, as memories of our mother's breast-cancer diagnosis and her quick demise came flooding back.

And that was when the school bell rang. I picked up my handbag and left. I went to see Patricia for an hour and gave her a hug ahead of her hospital stay. Then I went home, broke the news to John and cried. I sat on my patchwork armchair in the living-room and wept. That was how I'd spent my evening and when I came into school this morning with a fake Friday positive face, I was met with the horrific news of Callum's death.

Never in my life had I felt so helpless or numb. Even when my mother passed, at least I'd had my older sister, Patricia, to look after me. And I had my university degree to get busy with. But now, Patricia was gone to get cancer tests, which had never ended up well for anyone in our family, and it truly felt like nothing or no one could help me.

Callum… Words couldn't express my

feelings about what he did. A misunderstanding, an innocent mistake. He acted so quickly, made an irreversible, rash decision and there was no escaping the fact that he reached out to me before he did it.

He looked to me, his trusted teacher, for help.

Classes didn't go ahead that day for the sixth-years. The local priest came to visit and counsellors from the department of education arrived to talk to the students about their friend. Most of them were collected by their parents and went home. I couldn't be of help to them. I sat with the other teachers in the staffroom with my head in my hands, just like them. None of us wanted to teach that day. Callum was well known and had three siblings in the school, so most of the pupils knew someone who knew him and everyone was devastated.

Maureen and I brought our cups of tea to my office, just to escape for a few minutes. When she left, I cried. The sadness was unbearable, but the guilt was even worse. If I had followed up in some way after our meeting, then maybe someone could have reached Callum before he entered the garden shed. If I had phoned his parents to let them know of his distress, or told his class tutor, or asked one of his friends to check on him, then maybe... I was pretty sure someone could have intervened. Anyone...just not me.

*   *   *

I went home early and went straight to bed. I didn't even check in with Patricia. She'd probably have had her biopsy by now, but I didn't feel like talking. I've never not felt like talking to her before. We were closer than close, but the shock of Callum's death overwhelmed me. I knew Patricia would understand. She worked with kids too in the library and seemed to unconditionally love every child that walked in the door. She would understand why I didn't want to pick up the phone today.

The minute I heard John's key turn in the front door, I got up. Staying in bed hadn't helped anyway.

When he saw me appear in my dressing gown with messy hair and puffy eyes, he rushed over.

'Ah no, is it bad news about Patricia?' he asked.

'What? Oh no, well...' He knew how worried I was last night about her hospital tests. He just didn't know another tragedy had trumped Patrica's.

'I have to sit down.' He helped me over to the kitchen table and I sat. 'One of my students died by suicide last night,' I informed him.

'Oh my God, are you serious? That's terrible, Debra. What happened?'

'He was being teased by his peers for dating

a fourteen year old. He thought she was eighteen. He really didn't know and I think that's why he...' I put my hand to my mouth and cried.

'Teased? Only that? Sure, we've all been teased. Wow, that's extreme, isn't it?' He was stunned.

'Well, it was vicious. He was being called a paedo and the like.'

'Ah no. The cruelty of it. What are those teenagers thinking?' He shook his head.

'Well, that's just it. They don't think half the time. They just act. Or worse still, copy what their friends are doing. That's why they're called teenagers and not adults.'

'Hmmm. So, I take it, it was one of your students, then?'

'Yeah, a sixth year. Lovely guy. One of the best, actually. I was very fond of him.' I put my head down and studied our table cloth. It showed a map of the world, an atlas tablecloth it was. Guests loved it. We barely noticed it, until now. I searched for Mongolia for some reason.

'Sorry, Deb.' He placed his hand on my shoulder as he got up to boil the kettle.

'I don't want tea, John,' I told him. 'What's in the cabinet?'

'Oh right, yeah. Whiskey, brandy?'

'Brandy, thanks.'

'And what about Patricia?' he enquired.

'I don't know,' I said. 'I haven't checked in yet. There's something else, something about

Callum.'

'Who?' John asked.

'Callum, my student who died. He…he came to me the day before. He wanted to talk. He was, well, he was upset, I suppose. His friends just found out that his new girlfriend was fourteen and…actually, he only just found out too. He said he genuinely didn't know and I believe him. He's such a lovely student, never an ounce of trouble from him and then the first bit of drama surrounding him in his six years at Sacred Heart, and he goes and takes his own life. I mean it beggars belief. I just don't understand.' I stopped to wipe away more tears.

'And what happened when he came to talk to you?' John asked.

'Well, that's just it, John. Nothing! He poured his heart out to me, practically cried in my office and somehow, stupidly, I did nothing about it.'

'What do you mean? Surely you tried to talk some sense into him or put him in touch with someone, no?'

'I've gone through it in my head a thousand times. I've retraced my steps and my thoughts from the last twenty-four hours and I'm shocked to the core about how inactive I was. I started to try to reassure him, but he was having none of it. He stormed out of my office and disappeared. No one has seen him alive since, as far as I know.' My head banged on the table as it missed the cradle of my folded arms. I didn't feel any pain, but John got a fright.

'Jeez, Deb, steady on! Are you okay?' He seemed concerned.

I propped my head up with my hand, glad I had thought to remove my glasses earlier. 'Don't you see, John? I'm culpable. This whole thing could have been prevented had I acted accordingly and professionally. I should have told his year-head, warned his parents or even had a word with a sibling or friend of his. I could have prevented his death, John!'

'No, ah no, Debra. Don't blame yourself like that. You said the chap stormed out of your office. There was no stopping him. Sounds to me like he had his mind made up. If anyone's to blame, it's those name-calling friends of his. I mean you can't go around calling someone a paedo, can you? That's not right, is it? And what about the young lady who lied about her age?'

'John, she's not to blame. She's a child for God's Sake.'

'Well, all I'm saying is you're not to blame either. I don't want you doing that to yourself. Here, drink some brandy and have an early night. When's the poor, young fella's funeral?'

Chapter Three

A fter two brandies I slept like a log. Maureen was planning to open the school on Saturday afternoon to offer Callum's classmates a place to congregate and grieve together. She knew I wouldn't be there because she understood how hard Callum's death had hit me. I was excused from attendance along with three of his teachers who were close to him. How I wished he'd sought advice from one of them instead of me. But he chose me above everyone else. He trusted me the most.

When I checked *RIP.ie* I was surprised that no funeral details had been entered. There was no record of his death. I texted Maureen to see if she knew. She rang me almost straight away.

'Hi Debra. It's just one tragedy after the next, it seems. Callum's parents haven't entered his funeral details because word just came in that the young lady, Glenda, who he was seeing, tried to take her own life last night.'

'Oh heavens! Are you serious, Maureen? What happened?' More shock crippled me, and I had to sit down before I fell over.

'Apparently, she felt guilty about lying to him. The story is that when she heard about the name-calling, she broke up with Callum and it was a fairly public break-up too, so that can't have been easy for him. Then when she heard he died by suicide, she went and took an overdose. She's in hospital now, fighting for her life.'

'Oh Lord, Maureen, stop. Stop! I can't take it anymore. Text me when you hear of Callum's funeral details. This is all too much. Honestly, in all my years...'

'I know, Debra. It has shocked the whole school community, but we have to be the strong ones. We have to lead the way to healing after this tragedy. And we have to be there for the grieving students. Can you come in today, Debra?'

'No, no I can't.' That was my gut response. No one knew how guilty I felt about this whole thing, except John. But soon the questions would come about the follow-up care for the distressed student who confided in me. Soon the investigation would begin and I wouldn't have a leg to stand on.

Regardless of whether or not I'd followed up after our meeting, I still felt culpable. I should have been more forthright in stepping in. I should have done more.

The more I thought about it, the more I drove myself crazy. My racing mind was catastrophizing to no end, even though I knew the catastrophe had already occurred. As the guilt in my heart grew, I wondered if things could get any worse. I genuinely had no idea what I was going to do.

In an effort to cope, I tried resting in bed

or fixing myself a snack, but found I couldn't eat or sleep. The fact that I hadn't consoled Callum's parents was playing on my mind. By now, surely, they would know that he came to speak to me on the day of his death. They would want to know what was said. But I wasn't ready to confront them. I pulled out my laptop and typed a record of our encounter. A true record, ending with him storming out and me calling after him.

I cried when I closed my laptop. This was the worst thing I'd ever done in both my professional and personal life. I felt responsible for the death of my beloved student. I looked towards the drinks cabinet and spotted the bottle of brandy from which John had poured for me the night before. Just as I was getting up and moving in the general direction of it, I heard the key turn.

'John?' I called. 'Is that you?' I was alarmed. It was only one in the afternoon. Usually, on a Saturday, he played golf and wouldn't arrive home until early evening.

'Debra? Yeah, it's me. I'm glad you're here.' He appeared in the kitchen, brown coat still on. The same one I'd bought him ten years ago. He wasn't a spender and had no interest in fashion. In fact, I didn't either, so we were well matched in that regard.

'I was worried about you so I came home early. I couldn't focus anyway.'

'Ah John, you didn't have to. I'm coping well enough and I slept last night. It's just going to take a while to get over the shock, that's all.'

'I know, I know it is. Sit down, Debra. I have something else to tell you.' I'd never seen him look so serious.

I did as I was told and sat at the kitchen table. 'What? What is it, John?'

'Christy phoned me while I was on the golf course.'

I jumped. 'Oh no, I totally forgot to check in. Patricia? How is she?' I instinctively reached for my phone.

He raised his hand. 'No need,' he said. 'She's resting. It's been a long day.'

I looked at him over the top of my glasses. 'What do you mean, John? What did Christy say?'

'It's not good, Debra. They can tell already. The lumps are malignant. She needs further tests. They're keeping her in. Christy said she didn't get any sleep last night. He rang me as he was leaving her bedside and she'd just nodded off, so he said not to disturb her. They'll let her sleep and probably wake her up for dinner at around five o'clock. You could phone her then?'

'Oh no. I feel awful. I've been so…'

'Don't worry. I explained to Christy about what happened in your school and he sent his condolences. He said not to worry about being preoccupied and that Pat would understand. You know she will.'

I nodded. Of course she would. I knew that. 'I should try to get in to see her,' I said.

'Ah, Christy is getting everything she needs. He said she's exhausted and just needs rest. Maybe ring her later instead of going in. Sure, they might need you in school this afternoon? Or, eh, when's the funeral?'

I fobbed him off about the funeral. I told him the details hadn't been released yet, because Callum's girlfriend or ex-girlfriend was now fighting for her life in hospital. He saw how drained I looked and ordered me to go to bed. He said he'd bring up some tea and toast to me in an hour. Like a real hospital patient I was now, and John like my carer.

How the mighty have fallen, I thought, in disbelief as I trudged up the stairs. *One day, you're skipping into school full of the joys with keen expectations for the day, and the next, going to bed for the afternoon because everything happening around you is too grim to bear.*

The prospect of one or even two teenage funerals in the locality was too much. I didn't think it would ever be worth getting out of bed again. I took off my dressing gown, turned on my electric blanket at full blast and crawled under the covers.

*   *   *

John didn't wake me. He said he came up after an hour and I was snoring a bulldog. Our neighbour had an overweight English bulldog so we were familiar with the thunderous, grunting sounds. It was the first time he'd ever compared me to Rover, though.

He thought I needed the rest, given all the bad news of late. But I didn't and I wished he'd called me, because I was completely out of routine and probably wouldn't sleep a wink tonight. I went downstairs at seven in the evening. He was watching *Room To Improve*, a home-renovation programme. Silly old fool, I thought. I had no time for frivolous TV watching.

'Patricia rang while you were asleep. She's worried about you,' he informed me.

I could feel my face redden. 'SHE'S worried about ME? She's the one diagnosed with cancer for goodness sake. What's she doing worrying about me?'

'Well, when she heard all the bad news from your school, she knew how that would affect you and I suppose she realised how serious it was when she didn't hear from you.'

'Oh,' I looked down. Like a dagger that was, but John wouldn't realise. He knew we were close, but didn't understand the intimacy of sisters. Jeez, I thought, I didn't even ring her yet and she knew that I knew. And SHE was worried about me! I didn't know why the guilt didn't propel me to pick up the phone. It didn't encourage me in any way, it just made me feel even more listless, that was all.

I ate the soup John heated up for me and we watched the rest of *Room To Improve* together. I had to admit it was interesting to watch the dynamics between the builder, architect and home-owners. It was technical too, so I could understand the appeal for John. As for me, I found the dulcet tones of the presenter's voice somehow reassuring.

When it was over, John nipped out to pick up some bread for the morning before the shops closed. I checked my messages. Maureen had sent me the link to Callum's funeral arrangements, but I didn't open it. I put my phone down on the coffee table and went to the cabinet. I fixed myself a large brandy and returned to the couch.

I didn't pick up my phone. I flicked through the channels and sipped my brandy. When John got home I suggested watching a movie. He was delighted. We rarely watched movies and when we did, it was always John's suggestion. *Hope Springs* was starting on RTE1. John was a fan of Tommy Lee Jones and I loved Meryl Streep, so we thought we'd give it a try.

It didn't disappoint. We both got totally engrossed in it and loved it. We laughed and cried at the same times throughout. There was the usual amount of uncomfortable shifting on the couch when certain scenes portrayed the couple's failing marriage. While we weren't technically married, we could still identify with the apathetic complacency that pervades a longstanding relationship, if one allowed it too.

And we both did. We didn't fight the stagnation. There was no motivation to do so. I admired Meryl Streep's character when she stepped up and tried. I thought she was courageous and driven. My career seemed to consume all of my courage and drive. I had nothing left at the end of the day for John. And he didn't demand anything of me.

Afterwards, he asked me if I was okay and I said I was, even though I wasn't. He offered me another brandy and I accepted, even though I shouldn't have. He drank one to keep me company.

He asked me about the funeral and if I'd like him to come along for moral support. I declined, as I knew I'd have my colleagues for consolation. He accepted that and kissed me on the forehead before going to bed.

Little did we know then that it would be months before we'd see each other again.

Chapter Four

I found myself alone on the couch draining the end of my second large brandy. I realised I wasn't going to be able to go to Callum's funeral. If I couldn't bring myself to open the funeral link Maureen had sent, then I couldn't do anything related to his passing. I didn't want to sympathise with his siblings, face his grieving parents or see my sixth years in tears. I knew my colleagues could handle it.

I was lucky to be in a school with a tight-knit, supportive staff and I had full confidence in them to look after each other and the students. I just had no faith in myself.

I sat there for a while and wondered what I could do. How could I escape? Suddenly, Callum's decision started to make sense to me. The prospect of getting away from it all, not having to deal with people and not having to feel these feelings anymore held some sort of allure for me. I got a brief insight into the motive behind his final actions, but I also knew I wasn't as audacious as him and couldn't go through with something like that.

I briefly admired his courage, and Glenda's too, before snapping out of my trance. I looked down at my glass. Had the brandy gone to my head already? Why was I giving teenagers credit for ending their lives? Or trying to. What was wrong with me?

I got up and filled my glass with water, knocked it back and ran to the bathroom. After peeing, I washed my hands and stared at myself in the mirror. The bright light of the bathroom did me no favours. I had aged badly. The fine lines around my eyes and mouth were getting almost as deep as the creases in my forehead.

My glasses covered up my crow's feet to an extent, but my wispy, brown hair gave the game away and aged me beyond my early fifties. If it wasn't for hair dye, I'd have people offering to link my arm crossing the road. I'd swear most of the students and young teachers thought I was close to the retirement age of sixty-six.

My fiftieth birthday had come and gone. We had Patricia and Christy over for dinner, drank some champagne and played cards until two in the morning. Then I was fifty years old and nothing more was said about it.

My colleagues had asked if I was doing anything or going anywhere, like a cruise of a lifetime or something. I laughed and told them maybe we'd book a break away in the summertime. John had just chuckled and raised his eyes when I told him.

The truth was I had actually wanted to mark it in some way, but with the busyness of school and exam prep for the students, I didn't get a minute to do nice things for myself. With that thought, I went upstairs and took the suitcase from the spare room. John was a heavy sleeper so he didn't wake when I clattered it off the wall on my way back downstairs.

I opened the hotpress and filled the suitcase with clothes belonging to me. I grabbed a few toiletries from the bathroom and some snacks from the kitchen cupboard. As I went to get my coat, I realised I was still in my dressing gown. Like a woman deranged, I tiptoed upstairs and opened our bedroom door wide enough to let the landing light in. I took some more clothes and underwear, together with my sparse makeup bag. John was snoring softly, more like a pussy cat than our neighbour's bulldog.

I got changed in the bathroom and hung my dressing gown on the back of the door. That would be too bulky to bring along...to wherever the heck I thought I was going. I took one last look in the mirror and saw a depressed, sad, lonely, ridiculous old woman, and I said goodbye to her.

*   *   *

I didn't want to check my phone, because I knew the link to the funeral arrangements was waiting for me. I didn't want the temptation of opening it, breaking down and losing my resolve. My resolve to do what, I didn't quite know yet, but for whatever it was, I needed it to stay intact.

I didn't take my keys, just my purse and phone. With my credit card tucked in my coat pocket, I could go anywhere. Then I made a last minute decision to throw in my passport. I went out onto the street at four in the morning and started walking towards the town, dragging my wheelie suitcase along.

I asked myself what day it was. It took me a while to remember it was no longer Saturday night, but rather the early hours of Sunday morning. Good, I thought, there would be taxis around. Sure enough, ten minutes later, I managed to flag one down. It was probably heading to pick up the last of the night clubbers from the city to take them home. *Well, sorry stranded revellers, but I'll be taking this taxi tonight.*

'Where to?' he asked, not even batting an eyelid at the sad, middle-aged woman with a suitcase who'd just entered his cab.

'What?' I wasn't expecting to have to make a decision straight away.

'Where to?' he repeated.

'Emmm, em, the airport?' I said.

'The airport,' he confirmed.

*   *   *

I refused to question the hasty decision I'd just made. I simply went with it and pulled my suitcase along to departures where the taxi driver had deposited me.

Where to? I pondered as I perused flight departures. Was it even possible to buy a ticket at the airport like they did in the movies? Or did real life adventures have to be well planned in advance and sensibly thought out. I was about to find out as I approached a glamorous, airport employee who looked as though she'd know.

'Once you decide where you're going, check availability online. Most flights will have at least one spare seat at this time of year. And, yes, you could be on a flight in just a few hours!' she said.

Wow, not exactly the same as in the movies, but I could do this. *Now! Today!* I could buy a plane ticket with my credit card and travel to another country! I went to the list of departures, but there was too much choice. I decided to take a breather and sit down. I had to.

Hmmmm, where would I like to go? Where would I like to go? Emm…no, nothing came to mind, so I bounced back up like a yo-yo and read through the outgoing flights once more.

London seemed easy and manageable. Not massively exciting though, because I'd been there before to see the sights and take in a few shows like *Cats* and *Starlight Express*. However, it was many years ago, so I imagined there would be lots of new stuff to see in the city by now.

I briefly wondered if the brandy had gotten me seriously drunk, but pushed those thoughts away, because doubts would set in and I really wanted to go somewhere.

London flights were regular, every hour in fact, and it only took less than an hour to get there. Done! Decided! I was going to London. Not too far from home, yet a safe distance to escape all of the heartache and despair. I purchased my ticket and immediately went to the bathroom to throw up. No idea why... I didn't feel sick or anything. It just happened.

My flight was due to leave at five past seven. I bought a cheese sandwich and a takeaway cup of tea. *London, here I come!* I said...to myself. And then I said it again, like a mantra, possibly in an effort to inspire excitement about my trip. Or even to feel something, anything, but it didn't work.

Later, as I took my seat on the plane, I wiped away tears. No one spoke to me and I didn't make eye contact with anyone. This was a business flight with most passengers in suits, probably heading to the London office for the day. Gosh, I thought, I'd hate a job like that. Travelling was so tiring. I yawned, before remembering that I'd been up all night. Maybe that was why I was in bits.

*   *   *

An hour or so later when I got my suitcase in Heathrow, I checked my phone. John was up.

John
Did you pop out or sth? Thought you'd need a lie in

Shit. I didn't know how to reply, so I did what my mother always told me to do. I told the truth.

Debra

I'm in London

John

What are you talking about?

Debra

Heathrow airport, actually

John

Is the boy's funeral in London?

Debra

No

He rang me.

'What's going on? You're in London? Is this a joke?'

'I know. I know it sounds mad and it probably is, but you see, with everything going on and all the tragic news, I just had to…get away.'

'Debra? Are you okay?' The concern in his voice unnerved me. Did he think I'd gone mad or something? *Had I?*

'Yes, yes I'm okay. I just needed to get away from it all. Escape or something.'

'Why didn't you tell me?'

'I didn't know. I wasn't sure what I was doing, but I knew I wanted to get away, so I got a taxi to the airport and that's…well, that's the story so far anyway.'

'And what are you planning to do in London?' he asked.

Good question, I thought. I looked around. There were so many people and it was so busy, and everyone looked as though they had this hugely important purpose. Could I pretend to be one of them?

'I'll just go and check the flight-board now, John.' That seemed like a perfectly reasonable thing to do.

'So you're coming home, then?'

'Emmm.'

'Deb? What time? I'll pick you up in Dublin airport. What time?'

Just then, a loud announcement boomed, repeating the phrase—"Thank you for your cooperation." I had no idea of what I was supposed to be cooperating with and I couldn't hear John. He couldn't hear me either, so I shouted into the phone, 'John, I'll call you back in a while.'

And I hung up.

Who knew what the human mind was capable of? Especially when one was in shock. I didn't fully register that I was panicking, but in hindsight, I believe I was in a state of muted panic. While appearing to be in total control and convincing even myself that I was, I actually wasn't.

My mind was preoccupied with desperately trying to find escape excuses and reasons why I couldn't go home. I ended up telling myself it was imperative that I book the next flight I laid eyes on.

I worked so hard at this that I believed there were no reasons NOT to book the flight that seemed to jump from the screen. The one that flickered on the list of departures. Or was that just my flaky eyesight? I couldn't be sure, but I trusted the flickering, faulty screen nevertheless, and it became my motivation.

Bangkok, here I come...

Chapter Five

I missed a call or seven from John as I boarded my flight to Bangkok around five hours later.

I was stunned that I could book a ticket in Heathrow and just a few hours later, after a hot, cooked brekkie, board a direct flight to South East Asia. Aviation had progressed rapidly over the years without me noticing. I was too busy in Sacred Heart Secondary School to keep up with developments.

I really hadn't taken much advantage of the long summer holidays afforded to Irish teachers, until now. Although technically, it was still term time and I'd have to explain my absence for the next few weeks. I figured I'd have time to work out what I should do during my eleven-and-a-half-hour flight. I'd have to plan and plot a lot. Stuff such as what I should do about my permanent, pensionable job, my relationship with John, my sister with cancer and my grieving students back home.

Lucky for me, I'd brought a notebook. And more importantly, plenty of mini packs of tissues, because every time I thought about my situation a tear came to my eye. I sobbed a lot on that flight and didn't write anything productive in my notebook. I had no solutions to any of my problems. The young man beside me heard me sniffing and asked if I was okay. We got chatting and that distracted me from my to-do or never-will-get-done list.

His name was Samuel and he was a medical student taking the year out to travel. He'd already gone interrailing in Europe for six months and he planned to spend the next three months in South East Asia. He had deferred his studies for one year, as he had doubts about whether a medical career was right for him. I encouraged him and told him I thought he was doing the right thing. It was better to find out now rather than later.

His story got me thinking. My best friend, Mae, had a son, Seán, who had recently qualified as a GP. He was based in a shared practice with my regular doctor. Seán could gain access to my records if I gave him consent. I wondered if he could liaise with my doctor and organise a medical cert for my school to explain my absence. This was often the way it worked in Ireland. It wasn't what you knew, but rather who you knew. And I was best friends with Seán's mother, so I had an in.

We were only allowed three days of uncertified sick leave at school, and I was pretty sure I wouldn't make it home from Bangkok in three days. I scribbled that down as my first step in my to-do list—*contact Mae to check with Seán re sick cert.*

Having something concrete to do settled my nerves a bit. Samuel was ordering a glass of wine with his meal so I decided to join him. We ate without speaking, clinked our glasses to say "sláinte" and then fell asleep for the rest of the flight.

*   *   *

'Samuel? Samuel?' No answer. I must have lost him. Damn, I'd been hoping to share a taxi with him. He'd given me a list of hotels in the city that he'd researched. He said there was availability in a few of them and marked them with a tick. I picked one that had the word palace in its title and showed it to my driver.

'Baht, dollar?' he asked. That was when I realised I should probably withdraw some cash. My euros were no good to me here. It took ages to weave my way through the crowds in Suvarnabhumi airport and refuse all offers of God knows what. As soon as I got some dollars, I looked around again for a driver. It was so hard to work out who I could and couldn't trust. In the end, I chose Frank.

I thought the drivers down in Co Kerry were reckless until I experienced Frank and his constant racing to get to my destination. I told him six times that I wasn't in any particular hurry, but every time I said it, he seemed to speed up. I realised I had no control, so to avoid risking a heart attack I sat back and closed my eyes. I knew I was missing seeing the landscape and the sights, but I thought protecting my sanity was more important.

Frank must have clocked my inexperience—

he fleeced me. Samuel had said it should cost me no more than ten dollars to get into the city centre. Frank charged me fifty and I had no energy to argue with him. Once I saw the name of the hotel, I gave him the money and began to drag my wheelie suitcase inside.

At least the taxi had air con. The city didn't. I was overcome by the heavy heat, and sweating after the meagre two minute walk from the car to the hotel reception.

Before long, the receptionist worked out I needed a room for the night. When she saw the sweat running down the side of my face, she said -

'Shower?' I said -

'Yes please!' And she laughed.

'Air con?' I asked, making a blowing sound. She answered -

'Yes please!' and smiled. I smiled back, hoping we were on the same page.

Someone came to help me with my suitcase. This was a good hotel and I thanked Samuel in my head. The concierge came into my room and waited. I realised he wanted a tip. I had no small money. I'd only got notes of fifty from the airport cash machine. He didn't understand me and began to look cross. I reached into my purse and pulled out a two euro coin. He accepted and left.

I exhaled and locked the door before turning around to check out my room. Wow, it was tiny. I wouldn't stay here long, but it was clean and comfortable with air-con and a shower so it would suffice for now. I sat on the bed and took a few deep breaths. 'Debra Devlin,' I said aloud. 'You made it to Bangkok. What the hell are you gonna do here?'

*   *   *

'Finally!' John said before yelling at the top of his voice. 'She answered, it's okay, she answered. Deb? Where are you? We've been so worried.'

'We? Who's with you, John? Who are you talking to?'

'Christy, Pat, Mae and George. We've been worried sick about you!'

'Why? I told you I was okay,' I said.

'That was twenty-four hours ago, Debra! And you haven't answered anyone's calls. It doesn't take that long to get home from London.'

Then I heard Patricia in the background. 'Put her on loudspeaker, John.' So he did.

'Did you go to Buckingham Palace, Deb? Or Madame Tussauds?'

'Patricia? Are you okay? Are you home from the hospital?' I asked, relieved to hear her sweet voice.

'Never mind me,' she said. 'Tell us about your trip to London!'

'Em, well...' I didn't know where to start.

John interrupted. 'Will I come and collect you? I was on my way to the airport yesterday and Patricia told me to go home. She said there was no point hanging around arrivals if you hadn't shared your flight details. She said you might have needed a night or two away just to cool down, you know, with everything in school and that?'

'Yeah, that was a good idea to go home and no, I don't need a lift from the airport,' I reassured him.

'I don't mind, Debra, honestly. What time is your flight getting in?' he pleaded.

'Well, that's the thing, John. I've extended my trip.'

'Oh? For how long?'

'Well, that depends. Actually, could you put Mae on and take me off loudspeaker?'

Patricia piped up. 'No, no that's not fair. Share the gossip with all of us, Debra! What's the craic?'

I answered her. 'How are you, Patricia? I've been so worried. I'm sorry I didn't ring...' I burst into tears.

'Ah Deb. It's not as bad as you think. They let me home with a bag full of drugs. Enough about me anyway. What are you up to? And I'm gutted to hear about Callum.'

That set me off again. Just to hear his name. John took me off loudspeaker. 'Deb, Deb come on. Where are you?'

I couldn't put it off any longer. As soon as the tears stopped, I blew my nose and spoke. 'Bangkok,' I said. 'I'm in a lovely hotel in Bangkok.'

I heard a bang. Maybe he dropped the phone.

'John? John?' I called. The next voice I heard was Christy's. 'Debra? Are you still there?'

'Was that John or the phone falling?' I asked, with a little chuckle. That was the first time I'd smiled in a while.

'Here,' he said and must have handed the phone back to John. 'I…I don't understand,' he said. 'How could you be in Bangkok?' That was when I heard mighty roars from the room.

'Bangkok, Thailand? Send a postcard, Deb!' shouted Patricia.

'Bangkok? That's a midlife crisis, John,' was Mae's offering.

And—

'Well for some,' said Christy with resignation.

I heard nothing from George, but he didn't tend to be pass remarkable.

'Debra, are you serious? What the bleedin' heck took you there?' John was shouting now.

'A plane, John. Look, don't panic.'

*   *   *

After the phone call, I almost felt qualified to become a lawyer given the amount of justification I had to fashion in support of my round-the-world trip. I had to defend and make sense of every decision I'd made since finishing that second brandy on the couch on Saturday night.

I could of course understand John's alarm, Mae's anxiety and Patricia's childlike excitement about it all. It may have been true that I was still in shock to find myself sitting on a modest, yet extravagant looking, crisp double bed on the Khao San Road in Bangkok. I didn't want to mull over the reasons why I found myself here in fear of going mad or getting emotional again, so I went downstairs to get some food.

The hotel offered a selection of western food so I played it safe and went for burger and chips, figuring it was in or around lunch time. However, I vowed it would be my one and only western meal of my trip. I couldn't wait to sample the Thai cuisine, having been a fan of spicy food for as long as I could remember.

I looked around the hotel restaurant feeling strangely reassured by the number of lone travellers just like me. There seemed to be more tables for one than tables for couples or groups, so I felt satisfied that I wouldn't stand out in this city.

I also noticed the ages of the other tourists varied greatly. At fifty, I was definitely at the older end of the age range. It didn't make me feel out of place, but rather brought a smile to my face. *Look at me! I'm fifty, I'm healthy, I'm financially independent and I've never been more ready to explore and enjoy what life has to offer!*

*   *   *

It wasn't long before I began to have doubts. Following lunch I slept for eighteen hours straight, and that left me questioning whether I was indeed in the whole of my health. Would I need to change my life's routine to fit in sleeping for two thirds of the day from now on, or had the travelling simply winded me?

I sure hoped it was the latter. I showered and dressed in the lightest clothes I could find. Having checked the Bangkok weather forecast, I realised I hadn't taken humidity levels into account when I'd packed my suitcase. Nor had I realised it was the hot season.

I wore a light blouse and long skirt with sandals. I think the sandals had stayed in my suitcase since our last holiday to the South of France. I was delighted to find them. This was the only suitable outfit I'd packed for such a climate.

It made me wonder where I thought I was going. Everything else I'd packed was appropriate for the ever-changing Irish weather. I had trousers, socks, tights, a jumper, two cardigans, and a light scarf, along with underwear and toiletries. My first mission would be to hit the shops in Bangkok to pick up a few long, flowy skirts that I could wear with my sandals.

I studied the map in my bedroom to check where best to purchase the dresses. I hated the taxi journey from the airport, so I wanted to find somewhere within walking distance.

I had a hankering for a bowl of porridge as it was my regular breakfast at home, but it would be too hot for porridge and I'd promised myself to try the local cuisine from now on. Anyway, I'd never heard of Thai porridge.

I smiled at everyone I met on my way to

the hotel reception. About one fifth smiled back, but I didn't care. Nothing was going to hamper my positive mood. I picked up a few leaflets by the door and exited the hotel onto the bustling Khao San Road.

I think I took approximately three footsteps before a tuk tuk crashed into me. I screamed with fright and crouched down to check my right leg. All I heard was—

'Palace? Palace?'

I looked up at the driver wondering if this was the Thai way of saying—"I'm so sorry, mam, for driving into you. Do you need medical attention?" When I glared back at him in horror, he drove on. I stood there and looked around. No one even batted an eyelid.

I rotated my ankle to make sure nothing was broken and tutted when I saw the huge dust mark on my skirt. I walked on, approximately four more footsteps towards the other side of the street when a second tuk tuk bumped into me from the other side.

'Ahhh!' I screamed in horror. 'I take you to palace?' he offered. An elderly Englishman was passing by and noted the puzzlement on my face. 'Just say a firm no,' he advised and walked on with a wink.

'Oh,' I said. 'No,' I declared to the tuk tuk driver and he drove off. I looked down the street for the Englishman, but he was lost to me among the throngs of people. I wanted to cry. I felt so unsafe. I wasn't prepared for this. I knew nothing of this city.

I turned around, dodged another tuk tuk on my way back across the street, hung my head in shame and returned to the safety of my hotel.

Chapter Six

A s I sat on my double bed I realised how much I missed my patchwork armchair in the living room at home. The teacher in me chastised myself. *You didn't plan, Debra. You didn't research for this trip. That's why it's such a disaster!*

I charged up my phone and rang reception to check the wifi code. I began searching for how to go shopping on the Khao San Road. The Englishman was right. A firm no should be enough to convey the message that I wouldn't be needing a ride from every tuk tuk that passed me. I looked up the best markets to get the kind of light dresses I wanted and was satisfied I could get there on foot.

I would do some sightseeing and visit the palace, but not today. I needed some suitable clothing first. I also searched for flights within Thailand. A beachy island appealed to me more than the bustling city of Bangkok. I dithered a little and then just did it. I booked a flight to Koh Samui. This time I would plan ahead and know in advance where I was staying and what I was doing.

With a new-found purpose and vigour, I marched back out of the hotel and listened to the directions in my earphones to get me to the market. I held up my hand and made a stop sign in response to any offers of transport, or jewellery or handbags. It worked. Fake confidence always did the trick.

Two dresses and a trendy satchel later, I was ravenous. I found a traditional Thai restaurant and decided not to be too adventurous for my first Thai meal, so I ordered a salad. Again, my lack of research and planning came back to bite me.

Never in my life had I sweated so much through every orifice of my body. And that was after only one mouthful of grated carrot and green leaves. The sweat streamed down my brow, through my scalp and onto my thin, wispy, dyed-brown hair. What was on this stuff?

For some strange reason I tried to convince myself that I'd get used to the heat, so I forced myself to try a little more. But after a second mouthful of the seemingly harmless, traditional Thai salad, I worried that my mouth was so hot, it may never function again as a mouth.

The burning sensation travelled down my oesophagus and immediately killed any appetite I thought I had. I looked around and everyone else seemed to be lashing this food into them. I checked the menu again to make sure I hadn't mistakenly ordered an infernal, spicy salad full of hot chillies, but I hadn't. I'd ordered the first thing on the menu, simply named, Thai salad.

I picked up my napkin to wipe my brow and made my way to the till to pay.

'Yes, yes,' I bowed in deference. 'Everything was delicious,' I said, despite having left most of the salad on the plate. I pointed to my phone as if

I had an urgent call to make, paid the bill and ran out the door. I went back to the hotel, bought a litre of cold, bottled water from the fridge at reception and drained it dry by the time I reached my room.

Learning curve—more research required. If I was going to stay in Thailand for a few weeks, I'd better study the cuisine. No more salads until I trained my mouth to tolerate hot, burning lava. I showered, changed into one of my new dresses and ordered a tropical smoothie at the hotel bar. It was heavenly and filling. I didn't talk to anyone, but rather enjoyed my own company for a while and engaged in some people-watching. As a student of psychology, this was one of my favourite pastimes. Not to mention valuable research for my studies too.

I observed a stony-faced couple, which is not how one would expect to look on a holiday of a lifetime. I noted wedding rings so I assumed they were married. From their accents, I gathered they were from a well-to-do area in England. They barely spoke to one another and when they did, they snapped. Could it just be tiredness from a long-haul flight?

The young man sipping a beer to my left reminded me of Samuel, the medical student I'd met on the plane, except this guy had darker skin and black hair. I guessed he might be Italian, but he didn't speak to anyone so I wasn't sure. He was swiping vigorously on his phone. Was he on a dating app in Bangkok? I supposed *Tinder* and the like was global.

People-watching made me peckish, so I ordered french fries and took them upstairs to the outdoor terrace overlooking the pool to catch a glimpse of the sunset. It was a little crowded on the terrace and people-watching was no fun when passersby got in the way, so I observed the city sky instead. This was when I turned my psychological eye on myself.

What would others make of me, I wondered. I was fifty and looked my age, definitely no younger and sadly, quite possibly, a little older. Did people see a sad, lonely, unkempt woman looking pathetic, nosey and even desperate, while savouring her salty, french fries? I hoped not. I hoped they would see a serious, budding psychologist beginning a healing, midlife adventure. I hoped it was obvious I was here to gain insights and life experience to take home, and improve both my own life and the lives of others around me.

I took out my notebook and jotted something like that in it. At last, I had a purpose for my trip. I knew why I'd come. It was to be better, do better and help others. As the sun set and darkness fell, I unleashed a tiny smile. This was the start of something new in my life. Yes, this was definitely the start of something.

*   *   *

After a slightly rocky start, my trip to the palace

went smoothly. As soon as I veered off the Khao San Road, I turned one way, then another, before consulting my map. That was when a young, professional, Thai businesswoman offered to help me. I couldn't thank her enough for her assistance as she arranged, right there and then, a reliable tuk tuk driver to bring me straight to the palace without any of the unnecessary market drop offs along the way.

She admired the dress I'd bought on the Khao San Road the day before. I explained I had done enough shopping and wasn't interested in purchasing anything else. She translated my wishes and told the driver exactly what I wanted and didn't want. He nodded and very kindly helped me into the tuk tuk.

We drove for approximately thirty seconds before he stopped at a bespoke jewellers. He took my hand to help me out of the tuk tuk he'd just helped me into. I said—

'No thanks.'

He said—

'Yes, yes.'

I repeated what the helpful businesswoman had translated for me. At least that's what I thought she did. I didn't understand what had been said. Maybe he didn't understand either and just acted as if he did so as not to lose business.

I browsed the jewellery for the minimum required time. I had no choice. After about five minutes he made eye contact through the window and I reckoned that was the sign that I could return to the tuk tuk. It was very humid and the heavy, city air was getting to me. I just wanted to get to the palace, say I'd been there and get back to my hotel.

We drove for about forty seconds this time and stopped at a bespoke, menswear design outlet. I pleaded with the taxi driver to bring me directly to the palace but he insisted yet again. I recognised the stony-faced couple from my hotel. They smiled and nodded my way, which made both of them remarkably less stoney-faced. I acknowledged their greeting.

'We fell for that one, too,' the lady said.

'What do you mean?' I asked.

'Were you referred to your driver by an attractive professional who promised to find you a reliable tuk tuk driver?'

'Yes, she was so helpful...' And then I realised. 'Oh, I see, I fell for it,' I said. It didn't seem to matter how much research or forward planning I did. This city had a habit of getting the better of me.

Their names were Sue and Bob and they said they might see me back at the hotel later. I decided to revise my people-watching conclusions from last night. They were actually sprightly and friendly. It was probably just jetlag that had them looking so serious the night before.

We went to three more retail outlets and a temple before finally reaching the palace. I had to admit the round trip was worth it. I loved the temple and was blown away by the grandeur of the Grand Palace. An American tourist offered me her socks on my way in. She was just leaving. Only for her, I may have been refused entry as I was wearing open-toe sandals. That said, I noticed others wearing flip flops without attracting any attention, but it was better to be safe than sorry as the American lady advised.

I marvelled at the intricate architecture and felt vastly removed from the boring, brick buildings in Dublin. It was a far cry from grey, concrete walls and footpaths back home. I was glad I'd bought sunglasses in one of the outlets, as the dazzling colours surrounding me almost blinded me.

After a couple of hours of immersion in the extravagance of the historical buildings, my feet started to get sore and the heat was getting too much for me, so I went to find my trustee driver at our agreed location. I was sure I'd paid over and above what a metered taxi would cost, but I enjoyed the ride nonetheless and still believed the Thai businesswoman had picked a reliable driver for me. I felt confident I'd get home safely.

Bob and Sue were at the bar when I returned to the hotel. It was lovely to have some company for a change and I got the feeling they felt the same. Travelling on one's own was lonely, but travelling in a couple presented challenges of a different kind. I joined them for a small beer and they informed me of their travel plans. They were travelling around Thailand for three weeks.

The evening was easy and conversation flowed. I told them I was taking time off work to celebrate my fiftieth birthday and my partner would be joining me at a later date. Not entirely true, but easier than explaining how I'd come to be here. Besides, I'd been pushing that out of my head. I wasn't ready to confront those demons.

It was only when Bob and Sue opened up to me about the reason for their trip that I understood their apparent low mood from the night before. They had miscarried for the third time. Three babies lost in three years. Both in their early forties now, they'd booked this trip to help them decide whether to call it a day or try again.

South East Asia had always been their favourite place to visit, and they wondered if a holiday such as this every year would contribute towards easing the pain of never becoming parents, should they decide not to continue trying.

I wished I wasn't the type of person that people felt so comfortable confiding in. I wished I didn't always wear my counselling, teacher and psychologist's hat. But for some reason I couldn't escape it. When people conversed with me they instantly trusted me and more often than not, shared their intimate life stories after a matter of minutes. The amount of times John just had to walk away from group conversations because they got too deep too quickly. Without meaning to, I'd become thoroughly invested in a stranger's life and play a role in their decision-making.

John preferred to shoot the breeze with a quiet pint or a game of cards and let me do the socialising, agony-aunting or whatever our company asked of me.

Bob and Sue and their baby-loss story got to me. I wasn't rude or anything. I listened and sympathised, touched hands and hugged at the appropriate moments before excusing myself.

I went to my room and burst into tears. Hearing Bob and Sue's harrowing story reminded me of Callum's parents. They'd lost their teenage son. 'Damn it,' I roared. I played a hand in this. I could have done more. Could I have saved him? I screamed into my pillow and flung my notebook off the bed. This was the real reason I found myself here. Nothing in my notebook was true.

I hadn't come here to celebrate my fiftieth birthday. I hadn't come here to be better, do better or help others. I'd run away. I'd chickened out. Nothing this traumatic had ever happened to me before and I lacked the skills to cope. Despite all my counselling and therapeutic studies, I had insufficient knowledge when it came to advising myself. I could only counsel other people, it seemed, and give them the tools. I didn't have the wherewithal to help myself.

Chapter Seven

When I awoke the next morning I still felt like a fraud. I would have wallowed in self-pity for a lot longer only I had a flight to catch. Koh Samui was my destination. I read and researched as much as I could over breakfast.

When my taxi arrived, I donned my new sunglasses so I could close my eyes in the back seat without the driver noticing. I knew, well at least I hoped, I'd get to the airport in one piece and I didn't want to be traumatised by the journey, so I turned my attention to making a mental to-do list.

I planned to call Patricia and have a proper catch up as soon as I settled into the beach resort. Myself and John had been texting since our last phone call. It sounded to me like he was beginning to understand why I needed this trip and some alone time. He missed me nonetheless. I'd always been the more independent one. We both knew John needed me more than I needed him, but neither of us held that against him. Or me.

He'd also spoken to Mae's son, Doctor Seán, who had liaised with my doctor. I did a short video call to confirm the details and after a consultation with Maureen, my boss, a cert was formulated for me. It covered my absence until the summer break at the end of May and secondary school holidays were three months in duration, so no one was expecting me back at work until late August. John mentioned that the doctor had written something along the lines of trauma, distress and anxiety to explain my absence. That sounded about right to me.

While I knew I was letting my principal down, not to mention my beloved students, I also knew that my attendance record to date was impeccable and I'd barely missed a day in God knows how long. Maureen had always praised my consistency and that eliminated some feelings of guilt for me. She had even used me as an example for other staff members who took days off willy-nilly.

As for my students, they would now be getting a substitute and I reassured myself that it would probably be a young, newly qualified teacher with an abundance of ideas and energy, neither of which I possessed.

I was about to put down my phone when a message came in on the teachers' Whatsapp group in Sacred Heart. Glenda had survived. This news filled me with relief. At least the community only had one teenage death to mourn.

*   *   *

I was confused when I landed in Koh Samui. I looked around and wondered if we were just stopping to refuel or something. But no, the passenger beside me assured me with sign language and repetition of the word "airport,

airport" that we had in fact landed in the correct place. It was just that I'd never seen a wooden airport, or an outdoor airport, or such a beautiful, quaint building that served as an airport. I felt excitement build as I looked around. Wow, I thought, a garden airport...I hadn't lived!

I felt smug that I'd remembered to book my transport in advance. So smug, in fact, that when I arrived at Coco Beach Resort I genuinely felt like a seasoned traveller. I embodied an air of confidence as if I knew exactly what I was doing. All a lie of course, it was just a show so I wouldn't get fleeced again like I did in Bangkok.

It seemed confidence was key in this part of the world, and one couldn't buy that. Therefore, I was left with no other option but to fake it. And I found I could do that, quite well in fact.

The beach resort was spectacular and more representative of what I'd imagined Thailand to be. When I'd made the rash decision to come here, I hadn't been picturing unbearable humidity and perspiration, or being crashed into by eager tuk tuk drivers. I'd been dreaming of resting and reading in a hammock on the beach, sipping coconut cocktails. Therefore, as soon as I checked in and unpacked, I made this dream a reality.

I spotted the hammock from my window, grabbed my midlife-crisis fiction book that I hadn't yet started and awkwardly wound myself into the hammock as soon as it became free. As I sank into it and swayed from left to right, I smiled to myself.

Now I've arrived, I thought. *Now I'm content in this far off land and I can begin to heal.*

I had a long road ahead and I knew that. Who, but a traumatised soul in need of help, would travel thousands of miles away to escape grief and a funeral. At least I knew what I'd run away from. I had a basic level of self-awareness about my situation, and that was a start.

*   *   *

The next morning I met Amara. She was the receptionist and manager of Coco Beach resort. She radiated kindness with her welcoming smile and warm, brown eyes. After speaking to her for only a few minutes, I felt like I'd known her all my life. This sense of instant familiarity was a rare and precious thing as far as I was concerned, and once we got talking it was as if neither of us wanted to stop.

She explained how she was a native of Koh Samui and she had inherited the beach resort from her late father. As she spoke, she was simultaneously sweeping behind the reception desk and restocking printer paper. I was in awe of how she multi-tasked with such grace, but she didn't seem to notice my wondrous expression. Or, more likely, she didn't have time to notice it.

Amara was eager to share her knowledge of the area. She spoke impeccable English as she had worked as a tour guide in Bangkok prior to acquiring the hospitality business. She looked so young to me, but when she spoke of her work experience, I realised she must at least be in her thirties. She advised me about how best to spend my time here. She sized me up and yes, probably judged me based on my age, my alone-ness and obvious lack of fitness. She also admitted she'd spotted me struggling to get out of the hammock the evening before and sent two staff members over to lift me out of it. They were lifesavers and I'd thanked them profusely when I stopped seeing stars after my dizzy spell.

So Amara thought a cookery class would suit my fitness levels. She didn't suggest snorkelling or scuba diving or jet-skiing, so I felt she had a well rounded idea of who I was already. She signed me up and booked my taxi there and then. She told me it would be a fabulous opportunity to taste the local flavours and have some fun creating a dish of my own.

I was excited about the course and returned to my room to draw up a to-do list. My first priority was to call Patricia for a much needed catch-up. As soon as the time difference allowed, I got right to it.

'Deb! It's so good to hear your voice! What time is it over there in Bangkok?'

Oh gosh, I had so much to tell her. It was nothing but fun sharing with Patrica. She oohed and aahed enthusiastically and never once questioned any of my hasty decisions. I felt her support envelop me through the phone line.

It was a little different when I tried to get information from her, though. She didn't give me satisfactory answers to any of my questions—

'When did you say your next appointment was?' and—

'What did the oncologist say?' and—

'Can you explain exactly what that means, Patricia?'

She was vague and flippant in her responses and her main message for me was not to concern myself about her health, as she had enough interference from Christy on that front. They were her words. She just wanted me to enjoy every minute of my trip and send her the new recipes from my cookery class the next day.

We laughed and shouted down the phone line to each other just as we always did. It felt as though she was only a twenty minute drive away as she had been back home in Dublin. And it really felt as though she didn't have cancer.

The one thing I was reassured by after our phone call was that she had her husband, Christy, and he was on her case. He'd let her away with nothing and ensure she did everything the doctors advised. They'd been married for more than thirty years so if anyone could look after Patricia in her hour of need, Christy could.

When I found my notebook I made a note to check in with him at some stage during the week. He'd give me more information than Patricia and would deliver it in a less haphazard way. I knew I could count on Christy.

Patricia promised to ring John with news of my latest destination. I planned to touch base with him the following day anyway, but her phone call would satisfy him until then.

*   *   *

The next morning when my transport to the cookery class arrived, I cursed Amara. I thought we had an understanding. I thought she knew me, what with sending over the heavies to assist me out of the hammock, but no, she didn't. A motorcyclist arrived to take me to my class.

'No, no,' I repeated. 'I'm a nervous passenger,' I pleaded. 'I couldn't even open my eyes in the taxi!'

But they were having none of it. The motorbike owner was called Ned and he was a friend of Amara's. From his weather-beaten skin and strong accent, I deduced he was from Scotland. He did nothing but laugh at my protests and instructed Amara to give me a "leg up" onto the back of his bike. She did as requested because she didn't want me to be late.

I put my arms around Ned and held on tight. I closed my eyes for much of the journey, but he was kind to me and didn't race like the other motorbikers. He'd promised to get me there safely and true to his word, he did. I dismounted outside the cookery school chalet and he gave me a hug and told me I was brave.

It seemed I was already a laughing stock around here, but I was making friends and had people helping me and looking out for me. I was beginning to feel secure. I waved him off as he rode away to collect his next victim.

When I stepped into the chalet I was overwhelmed by exotic Thai aromas. The ones I could identify were lemongrass and coconut, but there were so many more. I introduced myself to the other group members. There were eight of us in total starting the cookery course. The mood lifted and any awkwardness dissipated as soon as our teacher made himself known.

Anurak was charismatic with a larger-than-life personality even though he was small in stature, roughly about five-four I guessed. He had shiny, brown skin and smiley, dark eyes that conveyed a sense of divilment. He was dressed in wide, striped, Thai fisherman pants and a high-collared, traditional Thai shirt. I hadn't seen such a bright, colourful ensemble on anyone since my arrival and I immediately knew this was a glimpse into his vibrant personality.

We sat in a circle on the floor while he introduced himself and gave an overview of the three day course. I was kindly given a firm, bulky cushion to sit on as I wasn't as flexible as the other younger members of the group. Anurak told us the meaning behind his Thai name. It meant angel and he assured us his "mama" had made a mistake with that.

He was funny and engaging and made the course sound like we were about to embark on a culinary experience that would change our lives forever. We started with a guessing game. He split us into pairs and gave us a blindfold. We had to guide our partners to the tasting table and pick up a variety of herbs, fruits and veg for them to smell. Then we had a competition to see which pair correctly identified the food items.

It was challenging and educational and like Amara had promised, right up my street. When Ned came to pick me up I was still beaming ear to ear. I kept my eyes open for the journey back. From then on I wanted to see everything, smell everything and experience every little nugget this island had to offer.

A mantra entered my head as I observed my surroundings in detail. *Let the healing begin, let the healing begin...*

Chapter Eight

John's messages were becoming more frequent. I understood. He was worried about me. And I suppose he felt lonely in the house without me. He kept demanding to know when I would be coming home. I had no answers for him. I only told him that I'd know when I was ready because I'd feel it.

He didn't appreciate the ambiguity. He wanted to know if I planned on staying somewhere for a few weeks. Then he could book a flight and meet me. It made me flinch when he said that. I realised that whatever I was feeling, it wasn't loneliness. I didn't miss him, but I couldn't tell him. I didn't want to hurt him more than I already had.

I put him off, saying that I was exploring and had no plan. That was true. I'd booked a return flight to Bangkok when I came to Koh Samui. But I had no intention of spending more time in a bustling city. I liked beach life. I liked island life. I liked Koh Samui and was willing to give it a chance. I knew there were other smaller islands too, but I was happy to spend more time here and immerse myself in Anurak's culinary experience.

On day two of the cookery course, we cooked! No more guessing games. We followed Anurak's recipe and instructions, and each group made an authentic Thai green curry with only slight variations in ingredients. We wined and dined that afternoon and I felt at ease with the strangers I'd just met at the course.

When Ned arrived to collect me, he recoiled in laughter.

'Look at you, Debra! Sozzled! I can tell!'

I laughed too and told him all about the curry I helped cook and the interesting lives of my new course mates. He said—

'So that's why they're here in Koh Samui. What about you? What's your story?'

Oh damn, I thought. Everything had been so jovial and light-hearted today. I resisted the call to get serious and explain myself.

'I've run away, Ned. That's all I'll tell you for now. I'm going to find my hammock and sleep off this curry. I'll tell you more some other time.'

'Intriguing!' he winked. 'I look forward to it.'

I did just what I said I would. I belly-flopped into the hammock, swayed from side to side for a few minutes and fell asleep for a couple of hours. Thank goodness I was under a shade.

People seemed to miraculously know when I needed rescuing. I didn't even call out anymore. They just sensed movement in the hammock and would come to my aid or else Amara would summon someone.

I showered, dressed in one of my new dresses and got ready for a light dinner. I wanted to try something other than curry so Amara gave me some recommendations. I ended up going for stir-fried pumpkin, *Pad Phuk Tong*, which was hard to say without laughing. I didn't mind dining alone. It was mostly young people around here who didn't take a blind bit of notice of me. I imagined the older travellers probably stayed in the fancy hotels. This casual beach resort suited me, though. I didn't want to spend all of my money too soon.

*   *   *

The next day when the cookery course ended, Anurak asked why I always seemed to reach for a colander during class and then do nothing with it. I told him that I only figured out that afternoon that he'd been saying coriander all along and not colander. I'd been wondering why colanders were such an integral part of Thai cooking. We shared a giggle about my misunderstanding and then hugged before parting.

He didn't know how much I appreciated him and his three day cookery course. It gave me something to focus on, something to look forward to and enabled me to get back to myself a little after the shock of what happened at home.

However, later that evening when I was alone in my tiny room, seeds of guilt that I thought were buried began to sprout. Callum's parents and siblings couldn't just escape to Thailand and partake in a cookery class for fun. No...they were still stuck at home in their grief, probably wondering what to do with Callum's belongings. Should they tidy his bedroom, read his diary or switch off his phone? They were stuck with those harrowing decisions and surrounded by inescapable memories of him.

These thoughts deepened my feelings of selfishness. I'd run away. I wasn't there to offer comfort to his grieving family or my dear students. I cried and cursed myself for doing something so joyous as a cookery class. Who did I think I was? And why did I think I deserved to feel joy?

With this thought I slept, endeavouring to make a decision regarding my next step when I awoke the next day. I wanted to be more helpful to others. I wanted to be of use to someone and not just rewarding myself with indulgent travel experiences. I knew, with a little research, my answer would come. But first, I would sleep on it.

*   *   *

Ned had a window because the cookery class was over and he had no morning pick-ups. He invited me out for coffee. We walked along the stretch of beach until we came to his favourite coffee spot. He called it a beach cafe but it looked like a little shack to me. The coffee paired with banana fritters was delightful, and we had both comfort and shelter on our wooden bench.

'I'm ready to hear your story now,' he said.

'Why? Why are you so interested, Ned?' I asked, wishing we could just shoot the breeze a little longer.

'Because you remind me of me. I escaped from Scotland many years ago, you know. And look at me—I never went back. I don't want you suffering the same fate.'

'What do you mean? Don't you want to be here?' I asked.

'Nah, nah, I've settled now and it's home to me, but it's not where I've always wanted to be. Myself and my ex-girlfriend, Vanessa, had wanted to travel and made huge plans. We decided not to settle down, get a mortgage and have kids like all our friends were doing.' He paused and looked me in the eye.

'Okay, I can see why you think we have stuff in common. I didn't do those things either except for the mortgage. I have a small house in Dublin.'

'Yeah, I noticed you've no wedding ring and for some reason I just knew you didn't have kids. I suppose you never mentioned it and that's how I knew. People with kids tend to talk about them, y'know?'

'Yeah, yeah, I suppose you're right there.'

'Anyway, myself and Vanessa said our goodbyes to family in Scotland and our first stop was Bangkok. We had a ball there, partying all night long and taking drugs. We met all the right people and the wrong ones if you know what I mean. Then when money was getting low, we took a flight to Australia because we had working visas. I got a job in a bar and Vanessa worked in telemarketing in Sydney. We loved it and travelled up the coast, went camping, met loads of backpackers and made friends. Our mates back home were dead jealous that we were applying for more permanent visas and hoping to stay.' He paused to sip his coffee.

'About six months in, Vanessa told me she was pregnant. Total accident—she forgot a pill one day. That's when our lives fell apart. I didn't want it. I didn't want to be a dad. I was loving life in Oz. But what surprised both of us was that she did. She didn't ever think she wanted to be a mum but when she found herself pregnant, she had a change of heart. There was no way she was gonna get rid of her baby. Of course, she didn't want to have it thousands of miles from home so she went back to be with family. I stayed.'

I noticed him welling up so I reached out to touch his hand.

'That was ten years ago. I'm thirty-eight now and feel like an old man. I still think of Vanessa every day.'

'Have you been home to see your child?' I asked.

'Yeah, I couldn't stand the guilt and I was still madly in love with Vanessa, so I went home to see her and our baby, but she…she, eh, refused to be in the same room as me. She told me she'd never forgive me for letting her go. Her family hated me too, but eventually her dad caved and let me see my baby, Scott. He was four months old at the time and slept for the whole hour I was with him. I… I don't know. He was like a stranger to me. A baby I'd never met and hadn't wanted, yet I was ready to be a dad to him if Vanessa would take me back.'

'Had you left it too long, Ned? You said the baby was four months old?'

'Yeah, while I was out every night in Sydney getting hammered, she was home in Scotland cursing me for not following her home. I lost my job in the bar for not showing up for work. I was drinking myself stupid. Couldn't live without her, but yeah, it was almost a year later before I followed her and that was long enough for the bitterness to fester. She really grew to hate me and didn't want me having anything to do with Scott.'

I waited until he was ready to continue.

'I had very little money at this stage, but I scrounged from my folks and flew to South East Asia. I lived there cheaply for a while, picking up odd jobs in bars and cafes. I tried reaching out to Vanessa and her family, but only got hate mail in return. Then after a few months, I heard she had a new boyfriend. This news broke my heart and I started drinking again. I lived as a functioning alcoholic in Bali for two years before getting help from a monk.' He burst into laughter, like the last thing he said took him by surprise. I got a fright and then joined in.

'A monk? Tell me more!' His story so far fascinated me.

'Yeah, he used to run a meditation group in the chalet beside the cafe where I worked, so we became friends and he saw how broken I was. Twice he found me asleep on the ground a few metres from my hut and dragged me inside to save me from the burning sun. He convinced me he could help me and I was in a bad way.'

'So what did he do? How did he help?'

'Cold turkey, I guess. He brought me to his monastery where he had trained. I stayed there rent-free, but had chores to do like scrubbing floors and washing dishes. I had to get up every morning at five to meditate with him. That's actually what saved me in the end...learning to meditate.'

'Wow! This is powerful stuff, Ned.'

'Yeah, I know that now. It took me a few years to articulate what I'd been through. My family and friends back home thought I'd gone mad or something. It was so unlike me to give up drinking and get up at five to meditate. I lost friends because of it. I suppose they just didn't understand what I was going through.'

'And what about Vanessa? Did she understand?' I asked.

'No, I think she thought I was doing drugs or something. I tried to connect with Scott, but of course he'd only heard bad stuff about me. My mum paid for me to fly home three years ago for my dad's funeral.'

'Oh, I'm sorry, Ned.' I offered my condolences.

'Ah, it's okay. I couldn't afford the fare. The

good thing that came out of it was that I met with Scott then. He's great, loves school and loves his new baby sister. I managed to meet with Vanessa and we reconciled. My mum downsized when dad died, so I gave Vanessa most of my inheritance towards looking after Scott. It was the least I could do. I only kept enough for my flight back to Thailand and I've been here ever since— meditating and doing odd jobs, but I have regular income from maintenance work in a chain of resorts. I'm like a caretaker now!' He lit up saying that.

'Well, you certainly cared for me since I arrived,' I replied with a smile.

'Yeah, how can I put this delicately? I always make a point of looking out for the more mature, lone travellers when they arrive. In my experience they're coming here with emotional baggage, hoping to escape from something or gain an insight into their situation.'

'Yes,' I agreed with him. 'Most likely, yes. If they're simply holidaying, they'd probably come with a partner or a friend, I imagine.'

We sipped the end of our coffee and observed the beach filling up with tanned bodies and beach traders advertising their wares. Then he looked my way.

'So Debra, now it's your turn.'

Chapter Nine

T his would be my first time attempting to articulate events to a stranger. I was worried Ned would judge me and never want to speak to me again. I didn't know it would be cathartic to express out loud what had happened. Up to now, I'd only really spoken to John and Patricia truthfully, but they knew me so well that they couldn't but be biassed in their feedback. Ned was more or less a stranger so I summoned every ounce of courage that I had to share my tragedy, and the part I played in it.

'I'm a career-guidance counsellor, Ned, in a secondary school in Dublin. I immerse myself in my work and barely have time for my partner of ten years, John. We go away to the South of France every year and socialise with friends and family during the year. We've no kids as I said. We met in our late thirties and soon after that John's mother and father died in quick succession. Before we knew it, we were both well into our forties and any notions we had of starting a family went out the window. I suppose neither of us wanted it enough to make it an issue.'

Ned raised his hand and excused himself to place an order. He returned with two large coconut shakes—my favourite! After a quick taste I continued.

'My job and my students meant everything to me. I wasn't just their teacher, they came to me with their problems and I always did my utmost to help them. Until this one time. I... I don't know what happened. I slipped up.' I paused to sip the fluffy whiteness in the glass before me.

'His name was Callum and he was eighteen. He was a diligent student. I knew his siblings and we had a great, close teacher-student relationship. Then one day he came to me, heartbroken. I thought it was simply that his girlfriend broke up with him, but it turned out it was more than that. She lied to him about her age. She was only fourteen and he thought she was eighteen. They'd only been together a few weeks and you probably know how it is these days—relationships are as virtual as they are personal. They'd only met a couple of times in their brief relationship. Anyway, word got out about her age and Callum was labelled a paedo. He took it all very personally even though it was most likely just teenagers shooting their mouths off and trying to be funny.'

I needed to take a few breaths for what I was about to share next. Ned sipped his drink while he waited.

'So on this particular day he came to my office, distraught. By the time I worked out why he was upset he got up to leave. I called him back, meaning to explain that we could sort out the situation and I could help him deal with the name-callers and rise above this temporary misunderstanding, but he marched out before I could say any of that. I had good intentions to follow up and arrange help for him, but that afternoon I found out my sister had breast cancer and I went straight to her after school. We're very close.' I said this with tears trickling down my cheeks and Ned patted my hand.

'It was the next morning that I found out Callum had died by suicide. I'd been the last person in school he spoke with. A while later I found out that his fourteen-year-old ex girlfriend had also attempted suicide and she was in hospital.' I wiped the tears with my hand.

'Luckily she survived, but as you can imagine, I feel totally responsible for Callum's death. If I had followed up with him, contacted his parents or class tutor, then, who knows? Maybe someone would have reached him and saved him. But I left it too late and there's no going back. I couldn't face his family or my students or anyone for that matter, so I booked a flight to London on a whim. And somehow, I don't even remember how, but somehow I've ended up here in Koh Samui.'

'Wow! I'm so sorry, Debra. Sorry for everything you've been through. I understand why you fled.'

'You do? Because I don't'. I genuinely didn't.

'You were scared. Your mind and body went into a state of shock and you did what you could to protect yourself even though that meant running away.'

'Oh,' I said. How cowardly of me, I thought.

'You came here because it's far away from your reality. You came here to figure out your next step. You came here to make amends. You came here to work out how you're going to help people like your student and his family and other victims of trauma. You're going to figure out your purpose.'

'Jesus Christ! Where are you getting this from?' I almost sounded accusatory.

He simply touched his heart. 'From here,' he said. 'I told you I lived with monks for a year. I meditated with them every day for three hundred and sixty five days. I've learned a little about human behaviour in that time. I see the good in you.'

'But...but didn't you hear me, Ned? I'm responsible for the death of this teenager. I was the last person he spoke to.'

'I see the good in you, Debra, despite what you think you've done. You'll find a way to resolve this for yourself, so you can move on and help others. Even help Callum's family.'

'His family? Sure, they'll never want to see me again. They'll hold me responsible for this. I'm half expecting them to begin legal proceedings against me and the school...'

'Debra, don't. Don't catastrophize about things that haven't happened yet. You have enough on your plate to deal with. Enough healing to do. You did the right thing in my opinion. This trip is going to change your life, because you're ready for change. You've been wanting change for some time now. I see a healer in you.'

I was speechless. I put my hand to my mouth and cried. He left to get me a tissue and then let me know that he had to go to work in a while. He took my hand, helped me up and walked me back to my resort. Before he left, I managed to ask him one question.

'Ned, what about Scott? Do you keep in touch with him?'

He pulled a folded piece of paper from his pocket. On it was a sketch of Harry Potter.

Ned laughed. 'We send letters to each other and now he can email me too. So yes, we're in regular contact. Vanessa has allowed him to visit his granny, my mum, at the weekends and they're getting very close. In a way, she's doing for him what I should be doing, but it's too painful for me to go home and see Vanessa with somebody else. It's been over ten years now since we broke up, but I'm still broken-hearted. Even with all the beautiful people here in Koh Samui, I haven't felt ready to move on or start a new relationship. But I've got plenty of friends and a meditation group and about six jobs to keep me busy.' He laughed again.

'Will you ever go home?' I asked.

'I'll go when I'm needed, like if my mum gets sick or anything. But I've got a solid community here so it wouldn't be easy for me to leave either. I take it day by day, hour by hour, minute by minute if I'm honest.' He reached over and gave me a hug.

'You take care, Debra. It's been a pleasure getting to know you.'

When he turned to walk away, I shuddered. I just knew I'd never see him again. And I missed him already.

*   *   *

I went online, frantically. If Ned thought I had a purpose, I was going to find out what it was. After scrolling and searching for two hours, I found it. Oh my word, I had so much to do and oh so little time in which to do it.

I ran to my room and packed everything I owned into my suitcase and handbag. I dashed to the reception to find Amara.

'Will you book me a taxi to the airport in the morning, Amara? And check-out...can I check out now to save time in the morning?'

She wanted to know everything and told me she would be clocking off soon so we arranged to meet for dinner. I promised her I'd explain everything then. I rushed out and jumped in the hammock for a quick nap after all that activity.

My snoring woke me up and by the look on the backpackers' faces surrounding me, it had entertained them for a while too. I asked for help out of the hammock and they obliged. I would miss that hammock, my peaceful sanctuary in Koh Samui. I would miss the island even though I hadn't explored it as much as I would have liked.

Maybe I'd come back some day to see more and do another cookery class, but right now I was on a mission. I couldn't wait to meet Amara for dinner and discuss my plans with her.

My inner bubble burst a little when I realised I'd also have to share my plans with John, Patricia and Maureen back home. Maureen would need to know that I wasn't planning to return to school in September. I figured Patricia would understand and support me even though she'd miss me. She might be disappointed that I wouldn't be returning home for a while, but she probably wouldn't let on. She always encouraged me no matter what.

But...John. I wasn't entirely sure how to share the news with him. This would be a challenge, maybe even a deal breaker. However, when I weighed up my options I decided it would be worth taking the risk.

Chapter Ten

A fter a final delicious Thai green curry I said goodbye to the lovely Amara, and gave her my email address to pass on to Ned.

The following morning at dawn I blinked away unexpected tears as I got into the airport taxi. Thailand had obviously impacted me in a deep, emotional way. From the multi-sensory experience of the cookery course, the comfort of Amara's homely resort and my brief, but meaningful, friendship with Ned. Even though my time had been short I'd packed a lot in and I was going to miss this place.

But nothing was going to hold me back from my next destination. Citywest Sydney University was offering the same postgraduate diploma in psychology as UCDN back home, except this one was face-to-face so it could be completed in half the time. This would mean finishing exams by Christmas of this year! And I discovered in my research yesterday that my course was transferable.

Professor Cooper, who was renowned for his mental health conventions, was associated with the university in Sydney and I relished the idea of being present at his lectures. I was a huge fan of his work so when I found out there were spaces left on his course, I squealed in delight like a true groupie. This course was like a fast track to my dream qualification and I honestly felt like this opportunity was uniquely designed for me.

But aside from all of that, I didn't want to go home. I knew that for sure. I wasn't ready to go back to how things were. I could feel myself gaining in confidence with every new experience of my travels. I was meeting interesting people and learning on the go. I was also avoiding going back to John. I wanted to put off seeing him for a while longer. I knew I'd have to make a call on our relationship sooner or later. I was just choosing later.

My plan was to travel to Sydney to complete my psychology studies in half the time, and eventually open up my own practice and give back, just like Ned predicted for me. After qualification I would go home to my own community and offer counselling, support and therapy to my fellow Dubliners.

I didn't know how this would make a difference to Callum's family, but maybe in furthering my education about human behaviour, I could in some way help explain Callum's rash decision and my despicable disappearance in the aftermath.

Glenda had been on my mind. Even though I'd never met the girl, I had a dream about her last night. She was dancing, doing ballet or something. Of course it was just a random image of a young girl, but in my dream her name was Glenda and she was fourteen.

I took out my notebook and wrote a note to email Maureen as soon as I got to Sydney to inquire about the young girl. How was she coping after her boyfriend's death and her own attempted suicide? I really hoped her friends stuck by her and that she had a strong family network to support her.

*   *   *

I finished my midlife fiction book on the long, arduous flight to Sydney. I slept and ate too, and that was about all I was able for. It was a relief to land in an airport that had no language barrier, or cultural barrier for that matter. I didn't bother with a taxi as I'd booked a hotel in the city based on the fact that it provided an airport transfer. It was just easier.

Sydney was a lot cooler in temperature than Thailand, which suited me. I'd get use out of those cardigans I'd brought from Ireland. Even though it was night-time and dark outside, I still thought the city was beautiful. Somehow, despite being thousands of miles away from Dublin, it felt like home.

I checked in, freshened up and tried to sleep. But because I'd slept on the flight, it took me a while. When I awoke, sunlight beamed in through the chink in the curtains and I felt a rush of excitement for being in a brand new city. I went down to the restaurant and ordered an Aussie breakfast, which was basically not that different to an Irish breakfast. I washed it down with some Australian breakfast tea, grabbed one of the cardigans I'd brought and set off.

Everything was much easier here, from paying with Aussie dollars to ordering food to eat. I understood signposts and my city map made sense to me. I walked around confidently, as if I was a seasoned traveller. I smiled smugly thinking that one day I would be able to call myself just that.

My first port of call was the City of Sydney Library. I briefly perused the women's fiction section. I always liked to have a book on the go. I found it comforting knowing I'd never be bored. Then I found a computer and began my mission of securing the details of my postgraduate studies. There was a huge amount of reading and research so I figured I could do all of that in the library. It didn't have to be in the university library as far as I knew.

I would need to be present three days a week for lectures and tutorials. The other days were for discretionary research, studying and shadowing live therapy sessions. I couldn't wait for that. Now that I'd completed registration I just had to find cheap accommodation in Sydney.

It wasn't long before I discovered that this was the challenging part. Hotels were just as ridiculously expensive as those back home, so I'd have to find a suitable budget accommodation instead. I didn't want to spend my life savings on high-end hotels. I'd already spent enough on flights. Fortunately, because I'd been signed off with a doctor's cert, I'd still be getting my teacher's salary paid until the end of August. This was funding my travels up to now, but it wouldn't last forever.

I wasn't having any luck whatsoever online so I approached the friendly-looking librarian. She was a middle-aged woman just like me and I trusted her completely the minute I heard her voice.

'Wow, I totally understand. The hotels in Sydney will eat up all your money. If you want to study here, you've gotta find a hostel or a budget hotel, unless you want to share an apartment with backpackers?' We both laughed together at that, knowing I was well past slumming it with youngsters.

'Hey, will you still be here in half an hour?' she asked and I nodded in response. 'I'm going on a short break and I can check with my colleagues. There's bound to be someone who knows someone with a flat to rent.' She beamed and waved. Wow, I'd just accidentally approached exactly the right person. I stayed scrolling in the meantime and when I took out my phone to check the time I realised I had a text from John. He had sent a goodnight text, but my phone had been on silent so I was only noticing it now.

John
I've confirmed 2 wks off Deb, starting next

Mon. Can I come over to see you? Miss you x

Oh, how I've mistreated him of late. He didn't deserve this. I should really talk this through with him. He generally slept like a log, but I sent a reply text anyway. He would see it in the morning.

Debra
Goodnight John, sleep well. I'll call you at 11pm Aussie time, ok? Chat then x

Maybe when I got settled somewhere in Sydney, I'd have a better idea about whether he could come to visit. I put it out of my mind momentarily and took a break from searching for accommodation. I decided to explore highlights of the city instead. I created a bucket list of places to see and things to do. I didn't want to leave Sydney unexplored the way I'd left Thailand.

In some ways I wished I could start over in Thailand. At the time I did what I could with my limited research, and to be fair, my delicate state of mind. But since my heart-to-heart with Ned I could feel my sense of purpose returning and I was slowly getting back to myself after all the trauma.

'Hi, sorry, I didn't get your name earlier?'

Oh, a half hour had already passed.

'I'm Debra,' I smiled.

'Sally,' she said. 'So I found someone that may be able to help you. Turns out this was perfect timing and you're in luck!'

She sounded super enthusiastic, but I had no idea what she meant.

'I spoke to Phil upstairs on the second floor and he knows of an apartment that's going to be available from next Wednesday. Apparently, one of the uni tutors from Citywest-Sydney is going on a trip to the states and his studio apartment will be available for the duration. Now Phil said this guy is looking for a house-sitter, just for maintenance and security really. He was adamant that he doesn't want students or backpackers because it's his place and he doesn't want it trashed, if you know what I mean.'

'Oh, yes, sure I understand. And did Phil speak to him regarding my query?' I asked, hopefully.

'Yeah, right there and then, he shot him a quick text. I hope you forgive me for being presumptuous about your age, but when this guy heard a middle-aged, Irish lady was looking for accommodation near the uni, he accepted straight away.'

'Are you serious, Sally?' There must be a catch. This was too good to be true.

'Yeah, yeah, Debra. It's yours from Wednesday for at least six weeks. You'll have to cover utilities and bills, of course, but he's only asking for $80 a week towards rental. He contacted Phil because he's too lazy to register for AirBnB and I don't think he needs the money. His trip to the States is fully funded by the uni, so it seems like he'd just rather not leave the apartment vacant.'

'Wow, well I don't know what to say except that yes, I'm interested! So what do I…?'

Sally heard someone call her. 'Oh sorry, Debra.' She checked her watch. 'I have to get back to work now. Come find me before you leave and I'll put you in touch with Phil. He works upstairs on the second floor.' And in a blink, she was gone.

Woah, how fortunate was I? She seemed trustworthy to me. I hoped I wasn't falling for some sort of scam, but my intuition told me I just happened to ask the right person the right question at the right time. I stayed and researched what I would need to begin my studies and picked up the book I wanted to borrow. This would be my last light read before starting the hardcore psychology books for my course.

I waited in line until Sally was ready. I showed my ID and was able to join the library and get a temporary card. I liked the space and the atmosphere, and was sure I'd come back to study once my course started.

Sally gave me Phil's number and told me to text him as soon as possible in case there was someone else interested. This was a golden opportunity and she didn't want me to miss out. I thanked her profusely and left the library with a big, stupid grin on my face.

I ordered frittata and salad in a trendy cafe nearby. I was blown away by the price of food in Sydney. I guess I'd been getting used to the amazing value in Thailand. I planned to tighten my purse strings until I found out for sure if this studio apartment offer was going to work out. If it did, I could relax a little then.

I left the cafe almost thirty dollars lighter and went for a browse. It wasn't long before I stumbled across the Museum of Sydney on Bridge Street. That was it—I stayed there until dinner time. It consolidated my feelings for this city. I believed I was falling in love.

I returned to the hotel and extended my stay until Wednesday. I cursed myself for forgetting to contact Phil. I dashed to my room the minute I thought of it and texted him.

Debra

Hi Phil, I got your number from Sally. I'd like to take the studio apartment near Citywest uni as soon as it becomes available. Please let me know. Many thanks, Debra (mature Irish lady!)

I showered, got changed and decided to have dinner at the hotel as I was tired from being on my feet all afternoon. I devoured every morsel of my fish pie and felt so at home in this city that I ordered a brandy to wash it down afterwards. That put me in the mood to lie down so I retired to my room for the night and fell asleep by ten thirty.

*   *   *

I awoke at nine o'clock feeling refreshed and

rejuvenated. I hadn't had such a peaceful sleep in a long time. I enjoyed a lazy, relaxed morning until I checked my phone. Seven messages from John and three missed calls. 'Oh Lord,' I muttered. He'd left the last message at what would have been midnight Irish time. It slowly dawned on me that I'd promised to ring him yesterday. I sat down and started massaging my temples. I felt so bad. After a perfect day in Sydney I'd gone and ruined it all by forgetting to ring John.

I checked the time difference. I couldn't very well ring him now. He'd surely be asleep. I felt rotten. John didn't deserve this. And I didn't deserve him.

Chapter Eleven

After breakfast I looked through my messages again and realised I'd received a reply from Phil.

Phil

> Well hello Mature Irish Lady! I can meet you at the apartment on Wed @9am. Address and details to follow, Phil (mature Aussie bloke)

Aw, that made me laugh. Thank goodness he replied. I had built my hopes up that this apartment would pan out. I finished the end of my breakfast tea and replied with a thumbs up. Now I only hoped that my message to John would go as smoothly.

> **Debra**
>
> John, I'm so, so sorry for not calling you last night. I fell asleep before 11. Can we call at the same time tonight? Please?

No reply. He must be conked out and a text notification wouldn't wake him up. He'd see it in the morning. An image of John briefly flashed before me—his thinning, blonde hair, his affable smile and pleading, blue eyes. I'd been avoiding addressing the status of our relationship. The reticence between us. I felt it. It wasn't just the current miles either. The distance had been building for a while.

It was a beautiful sunny morning in Sydney. I inquired at reception as to the best way to get around the city to do some sight-seeing. I wanted to see the Opera House and climb the Sydney Harbour Bridge. I remembered my friends back home, George and Mae, had taken a trip to Australia and Mae had raved about the bridge excursion.

The receptionist was friendly and efficient, but in no way as warm as Amara back at the beach resort in Koh Samui. I remembered how when I'd met her, I'd instantly felt part of the resort family, like one of the team. She had such an easy way about her. No wonder many of the holidayers stuck around for longer than intended. I'd only left the place last week and was already looking back with nostalgia.

It wasn't that I was pining to go back or anything. I knew in my heart I was in the right place at this time. But I marvelled at how badly I'd needed to feel part of a community, and Amara gave me that, even if it was only for a few days. I'd been so alone since experiencing the trauma of Callum's passing.

I thought of the night I left my house with John tucked up in bed. In the middle of the night I wandered the street where we'd lived for ten years. With lights out and everyone asleep, I'd felt so alone despite being surrounded by loved ones, friends and neighbours.

I supposed it was just my frame of mind. Nothing or no one could have penetrated me. I was suffering from shock and of course, loaded with brandy too. I really didn't know how I managed to make it to the airport and get on a flight in one piece. Maybe I'd analyse my behaviour during my upcoming course. I could make an example of what can happen when one gets blinded by a traumatic event and falls into a state of muted panic. Or something to that effect...

Anyway, it just reminded me how important it was that Amara had made me feel so welcome. I smiled while remembering how she'd sent help to get me out of the hammock, advised me on suitable food options and found exactly the right cookery class for me to indulge my senses and meet interesting people. She knew Anurak would ensure I had a blast. And she was confident Ned would look after me. She knew practically everyone on the island.

I was so glad I stayed in her humble beach resort rather than a fancy hotel like most travellers of my age did. Amara and Ned made my trip to Koh Samui special and I wouldn't have met them had I not ventured outside my comfort zone.

Just reflecting upon recent events was both enlightening and gratifying, because it reminded me that I was still learning something new every day, even in my fifties! I hoped this would remain the case forever.

*   *   *

The next few days in Sydney were filled with oohs and ahhs. Everywhere I went exceeded my expectations. My favourite moment was sipping a glass of prosecco overlooking the Opera House. I felt like I was in a postcard. I took lots of photos and sent them to Patricia and Mae. They both complimented my elegance and sent starry-eyed emojis in return.

My most exciting activity was climbing the Sydney Harbour Bridge. The guide's gregarious personality reminded me of Anurak. I got the same vibes from him and knew from the get-go that he was going to make this experience fun. He began by asking each of us to sing a song from our country.

He broke the ice by offering to sing first. He belted 'I should be so lucky' by Kylie, and did his best to channel a very high-pitched version of Kylie's voice. With his twerking and over-the-top hair flicks of his non-existent hair, he had all of us in stitches by the second line.

I made the mistake of catching his eye and he took that to mean I was ready to go next. Still laughing after his exuberant performance, I smiled my way through the first verse of 'Molly Malone' and everyone joined in with the chorus. When a tear came to my eye, it surprised me. I didn't think I was homesick, but singing this song with a bunch of strangers made me feel immensely proud.

When a Swedish family sang 'Dancing Queen' we joined hands and danced in a circle. We were beginning to attract a lot of attention from passersby, but this only made us sing louder.

Our euphoria skyrocketed when a pair of Welsh sisters sang 'It's not unusual' by Tom Jones. They were like a professional tribute act with all the moves and earned us huge cheers and a round of applause from onlookers. And all of this happened before we even set foot on the bridge!

We stumbled and struggled together, belly laughing all the way, especially when the Welsh sisters wouldn't stop singing. But we felt a huge sense of achievement at the end and I would treasure the photos from that excursion forever.

I ended up having dinner with the Welsh sisters afterwards and we agreed to keep in touch. We exchanged numbers and I'd already received some funny texts from them. I was glad I'd done the tourist thing because I knew once I started my course, it would be intense and I'd have no time for sight-seeing.

I'd also managed to reach John the day after I missed his calls. He sounded cranky and tired and said he'd been worried about me. Firstly, I apologised, but I could tell from his silence that he didn't readily accept. Then I tried to explain that I'd been suffering from shock when I booked the flights and only came back to myself in Koh Samui. That was when I started to see straight and began to plan for what I would do and how to make the best use of my time away.

He listened to everything I said, but his main question that he asked time and again was—

'And how do I fit into your plans?'

There was no easy way to tell him. He didn't. He didn't fit into my current plans at all.

'Look John, give me this time, okay? I don't want you coming to Sydney or anything. My course starts on Monday and from then on I'll be throwing myself into that one-hundred-percent. I wouldn't have time for you if you visited next week.'

'Sounds like you wouldn't MAKE time for me,' he responded.

'I'm sorry, John. This is just what I have to do. I feel like I have a lot to make up for and this is the start of it. I need this training to make a proper go of it. And, although I'm not ready to go home just yet, I want to open my own practice when I return. I need to get qualified first and gain some experience. I want everything to go smoothly. No more drama, you know what I mean?'

'Well you created the drama, Debra, by disappearing. The neighbours and, well, everyone is asking for you.'

'Oh. I hadn't thought about that. And what have you told them?' Sounded like I'd really landed him in it.

'I said that you were so upset about the passing of one of your students that you needed some time out. Then when they asked where you were, I said you were staying with a friend in London. I didn't want to give away all of your business and tell them you'd gone all the way to bloody South East Asia.'

'I'm sorry, John. I don't expect you to lie for me. You can tell the truth now. I'm on leave from work to further my studies in an Australian university,' I clarified for him.

'But that's not technically true, Debra. You've been signed off on sick leave. What's going to happen in September? What then? They'll stop paying you if you take a career break. Are you gonna quit?'

'No, well I don't know. As soon as I get settled in my new place, I'll arrange a call with Maureen and apply for leave in September. Don't worry about me. I'm excited to start this course. It's something I've wanted to do for a long time and I feel like now I'm on the fast track.'

'Could you not defer it, Deb? Come home. I need you, Patricia needs you...'

'Patricia? I spoke to her the other day and she sounded well. Why does she need me?'

'Ah, you know. Just the shock diagnosis and you two are so close,' he said.

'She actually encouraged me to stay here, John, and follow my dreams,' I informed him.

'Yeah, she would. That sounds like Patricia alright,' he acknowledged.

'But John, listen. I'd still like you to do

something nice with those two weeks off work. Why don't you visit your brother in Poland? Help him with the house plans. Spend time with Michael and Ewa?'

His brother had married a Polish woman, Ewa, and they'd recently relocated to Poland as she wanted to be close to her ageing parents. They were building a house on her parents' land and John was getting regular updates of the progress. I knew he'd love to see the work being done and he could stay with them in their rented house and catch up with his niece and nephew. He paused for a while. He was a thinker. That was my favourite quality about him.

'I'll see, Debra. I just wish you could come too, though.'

'I know. Next time. I'll be home before Christmas, you know. This course is only five months long. Give them my regards, won't you? And get the kids something nice. Ask Patricia what they'd like. John?' More silence.

'Okay, Debra,' he said with resignation.

'I'll let you go now. Get a good night's rest and, again, I'm so sorry about forgetting to ring last night.'

We left it like that. With me giving him a challenge to book a flight to Poland and bond with his family over there. I knew he'd love a trip like that and his brother would be delighted to see him. It would be good for him to get away. I could vouch for the benefits of travel. Being around the house just reminded him of me and made him lonely. This trip would be therapeutic for him. I could feel it.

*   *   *

I got up early on Wednesday morning to check out of my hotel. I didn't bother with breakfast as I was due to meet Phil in a cafe at nine. Since I'd be lugging my suitcase along with me, I decided to book a taxi rather than struggle with it on public transport. With a heart full of excitement I left the city and travelled west.

After parting with a small fortune for the taxi fare, I arrived at the agreed cafe a few minutes before nine. As I ordered bacon and eggs I realised this was a cafe with regular prices for its food, and not extortionate like most of the eateries in the city I'd just left.

I was ravenous so I tucked into my food immediately. I only looked up five minutes later when a booming voice startled me. 'G'day Boss, what a game last night, eh?' And then a boisterous laugh followed. It belonged to a tall man with a mop of curly, grey hair dressed in casual jeans and a t-shirt. A short chat about the game ensued and then the big guy turned around.

'Anybody know where I can find a mature Irish lady?' he roared with his thick Aussie accent.

I burst into laughter, almost spilling my tea as I raised my hand. He laughed again, that same infectious laugh that seemed to put a smile on just about everyone's face in the cafe.

'Debra?' he shouted, unselfconsciously. Now everyone in the cafe and for a few miles down the street knew my name! 'I'm Phil, nice to meet you,' he introduced himself as he walked towards me. 'Mind if I take a seat?' He pulled out the chair opposite me, still smiling. I couldn't help but smile back.

'Nice to meet you too, Phil,' I said.

Chapter Twelve

S o that was the beginning of the whirlwind called Phil. He ordered the same breakfast as me, gobbled it up in five minutes and emptied his coffee into a takeaway cup on the way out. We walked for five minutes until he stopped, turned and pressed a few digits into a buzzer code box on the wall.

'Oh! Is this it?' I finally managed to get a word in. Since he'd sat with me in the cafe he hadn't stopped talking. He told me where to get the best coffee, the most authentic pasta, the hottest curry and the creamiest Guinness. He knew everything there was to know about this part of town. I wondered if he grew up here or if he simply knew everything about this city because he worked at the library. I didn't get the chance to ask though, because he talked non-stop.

'Yes, Debra! Welcome to your new living quarters for the next six weeks! Right next to the university too.' He pointed down the street. I leaned back to catch a glimpse but he'd already unlocked the door and was holding it open for me.

'Here, let me,' he said and took my suitcase. 'Stairs, no lift I'm afraid.'

'Oh, I see. What floor?' I asked, thinking this might help get me fit.

'Two, Debra, second floor. Kinda windy

stairs though, as you can see. C'mon, we're nearly there.'

Jeepers, this man was like lightning! I struggled to keep up. He was definitely the least librarian-ish librarian I'd ever met.

'Are you with me, Debs?' He shouted down the stairs.

'Coming Phil!' I called back. Debs? I thought. No one ever called me Debs. I was Debra or Deb to family and friends back home. *Hmmmm, Debs...*

'So this is it! What d'you think? Do you like it?' He asked, before I'd even made it to the door.

'Emm, let me get in to have a look, Phil.' He stepped aside and gestured for me to pass him.

'Oh well, this is, well, this is nice. Cozy and...'

'I know it's a bit small, right? Studio apartments tend to be. What size is your apartment back home in Ireland, Debs?'

'My what? Oh, back home. Em well, I actually have a small two-bed house in Dublin, Phil, and it's quite spacious. But there's no comparison between a house and a studio apartment. I've just been to Thailand where my single rooms were less than half this size, so this is perfect, actually. Yeah...' I took one more look around. 'It's perfect!' I looked his way and we locked eyes and smiled. He seemed genuinely chuffed that I liked the place.

Then he left my suitcase down and went around checking taps and plugs and light switches.

'All okay, Phil?' I asked, trying to follow the pace of him with my eyes. He seemed to be everywhere all at once. Again, even though I wasn't moving, I couldn't keep up.

'Yeah, yeah, all seems fine. The guy that lives here, Marcus—he's a top bloke. He would've let me know if there were any problems.'

'Well, it's plain to see he looks after it from the condition he left it in. Thanks, Phil. I feel so lucky to have landed myself here. I mean, if it weren't for Sally... I don't know, I suppose I just met the right person at the right time and asked the right question!'

We both smiled.

'Everyone deserves a bit of good luck from time to time, right?' he said.

I nodded, sadly, unsure of whether or not I was deserving after recent events.

'All okay, Debs?' He must have noticed how my smile faded.

'Hmmm? Oh yes, yes, all okay. I was just thinking about something. So, em, what do I owe you and how do I pay for this place?' I changed the subject.

'Yeah, yeah, I have Marcus's bank details. I guess a bank transfer would work? Give him two weeks in advance and he'll be in touch regarding bills on top of that. Actually, he left a folder on the table with some info if you want to take a look.'

'Oh great, he's very organised. Well, em, thanks, Phil. Thanks for all your help in setting this up. I hope I'm not keeping you?' He was hovering by the door.

'No, no, not at all. I'll let you get settled in. And eh, you have my number if there's any problems like explosions or floods or if the toaster doesn't work.'

I caught his eye and we both chuckled.

'Okay then, I know how to reach you and thanks again.'

'Yeah, take care, Debra.' He smiled, nodded his head and left.

I stood there looking at the closed door for a minute. Was I half expecting him to barge back in with his larger-than-life personality? When nothing happened, I began looking around. Marcus had locked a few drawers where he must have left personal items. The kitchen looked well stocked with appliances and utensils and the info about the shared laundry room in the basement was very concise. Yes, I think I had everything I would need.

I couldn't help smiling to myself again as I looked towards the door. I wouldn't mind if Phil did come back. His aura had filled the room with something I wasn't used to. I actually think I might have started to miss him, even though he'd only left a few minutes ago.

I unpacked and hung my clothes in the narrow wardrobe. Marcus had left a tiny space and two free drawers which was just about enough for me. There was a chair by the window in the bedroom which caught my eye. I grabbed the biscuits I'd taken with me from the hotel room in Sydney and sat down by the window. It was overlooking a busy street and I liked that I felt part of it. I decided to read my book for a while and have a nibble of my biscuits.

I got distracted thinking of Phil's gargantuan entrance into the coffee shop. I'd heard him and felt his presence before I even looked up to see who the voice belonged to. I got back to my book and ended up finishing it in a couple of hours. It was about second chances and finding love later in life, a common theme in women's midlife fiction.

I realised I was starving so I showered, got changed and went shopping to stock up the tiny fridge. I just bought essentials and fitted everything into Marcus's two cloth shopping bags he'd thoughtfully hung by the door.

When I returned I cooked for the first time since the Thai cookery class. How I missed Koh Samui, although my time there had been short. I should have bought curry ingredients and tried to emulate the one I made there. Instead, I'd bought mince, veg, herbs, passata and other spag bol ingredients. I began chopping and frying, and boiling water for pasta. There was no TV so it was quiet. I could have done with some background noise. Maybe Marcus used his laptop for entertainment and had taken it with him.

I made enough food for the next day too.

I gobbled down a huge portion and then made a list of info I needed from the university. I was planning to go and visit it the following morning. After I cleaned up and opened up every drawer and cupboard to check if I'd missed anything, I decided to take a walk. I couldn't remember the name of the pub Phil had mentioned that served the creamiest Guinness, but I thought I remembered where he said it was.

I brushed my hair, put some lipstick on and grabbed my cardigan for a stroll. I walked for a half hour before I found it. It was actually quite close to my apartment so I had to back-track. I enjoyed the evening stroll anyway. I wasn't going into the pub to sample the Guinness that Phil had recommended. I'd get a brandy instead.

And I also remembered he'd mentioned he lived around here, so there was a chance he might pop out for a drink too. A slim one, but if he happened to arrive it might be nice to have a drink with him, I thought...

*   *   *

It was an Irish pub called Mick O'Shea's and had a decent crowd in it for eight o'clock on a Wednesday evening. There was a bit of background music too, which I was glad of, because it had been so quiet in my apartment. I spotted a newspaper on the bar and took it with me to a table in the corner. My hot brandy was soothing and helped me relax.

I sipped it slowly and read the paper cover

to cover. I considered getting another brandy but thought better of it since I didn't yet know the area too well. Besides, it was already dark outside so I decided to go home for fear of the unknown. The barman nodded to me on my way out. It was a nice, friendly local and I felt sure I'd come back.

I double-checked directions on my phone to bring me back to my apartment, as I didn't want to repeat the roundabout route that brought me here. Google maps told me it was only a ten minute walk so I set off.

'You have arrived at your destination!' A booming voice behind me frightened me and I nearly dropped my phone. I turned around.

'Oh Phil, you frightened the life out of me!' He really did.

'Are you lost? I saw you were checking maps,' he said.

'Oh no, I know the way back now. I came via a different route but it took a lot longer. I'm going to take a shortcut home.'

'Home? Debra, it's only nine o'clock! C'mon, I'll take you for a drink in my local…'

'Oh no, I've just been there. I had a brandy and read the paper. It's very nice. I'll definitely come back.'

'Yeah, you will!' He held out his arm for me to link with a big, silly grin on his face. I laughed and wove my arm through his. I couldn't resist his offer. We walked with linked arms until we got to the pub I'd literally just left.

'After you,' he bowed. It seemed everything he did made me smile. When we entered the pub, all I heard was 'Hey Phil', 'Alright Phil?' or 'G'day mate' and that was only the customers. When the barman saw us, he hollered, 'Hey mate, you're late!' And then planted a pint of Guinness on the bar for him. Before I even opened my mouth he said, 'Another brandy, princess?'

Bloody hell, I thought, was he for real with his "princess"? I looked towards Phil. 'He's kidding, don't mind him,' he assured me and winked. 'But eh, brandy, yeah?'

'Okay, yeah, the first one was good, so why not?' I shrugged.

'That's the spirit, Debra!' And we caught each other's eye and laughed again.

*   *   *

It was well after midnight by the time I got home. Phil had flagged down a cab for me after I refused his offer to walk me home. It was out of his way. He lived a ten minute walk in the opposite direction. I smiled all the way home in the extremely short cab journey, remembering how the conversation had flowed all night in the pub. And our laughter had become hysterical when Phil realised I thought he was a librarian. Turned out he was the maintenance technician in the library and in a few other state-run buildings across the city.

That made way more sense to me. He didn't come across as a librarian or an academic. I wasn't sure why I felt that way about him. Maybe he seemed too carefree? Whatever it was, I liked him and enjoyed every second of our time together. He was easy company and we made each other giggle like teenagers.

It was an exciting night too because everyone knew Phil and liked him. No one passed our table without stopping to say hello and chat about the "footy", or local news or to ask about his travel plans. He told me he takes time off every year to go travelling. He'd been to every inch of Thailand so we talked extensively about that. He knew of each place I mentioned, even the hotel in Bangkok.

We didn't get personal, so I didn't find out if he had kids or a partner and he didn't grill me either. We kept it light and he introduced me to everyone who stopped to chat. It was a lively, pleasant evening and I took note of the fact that he mentioned he "stops by" his local pub twice a week. He was a creature of habit in many ways, he said, so that led me to believe he'd be stopping by again next Wednesday.

I just wondered if I could wait that long...

Chapter Thirteen

I refrained from popping into Mick O'Shea's again on my own for fear of appearing desperate. I did think about Phil and fantasised about bumping into him at the coffee shop, or the supermarket or the local park. But there was no sign of him. If I'd nailed down which weekend night he went to the pub, then maybe I would have popped my head in, but I had no clue so I decided to hang on until Wednesday.

It wasn't like I had nothing to do. Besides discovering the nearby amenities, stocking up on supplies for my apartment and catching up with everyone back home, I also had books to find and stationary to buy for my course. I rented a laptop for a small fee from the university and borrowed the books I would need to keep costs down. On Sunday evening as I was packing a bag in advance of my first day at uni, I got a text.

Phil
Good luck tomor, Phil

I read it and reread it at least twenty times. Each time fireworks exploded in my heart. It was giving me palpitations so I sat down. I felt seventeen again. I beamed and clutched my phone to my heart. I was starting uni the next day and behaving more like a teenage first year than a fifty-year-old, mature student topping up a post grad. What was I like?!

And what did this mean? Was it just the excitement of starting something new and going back to university that had me acting like a student again? Or was it Phil? Had he awakened something in me? Something long forgotten. Feelings I didn't realise I still had. I knew I liked him and I'd been thinking about him a lot since I'd met him last Wednesday, but why had his simple good luck message stirred so many emotions in me?

I made some tea and sat down at the kitchen table to recover. When my heartbeat returned to normal, I picked up my phone and texted him back.

Debra
Thanks Phil, I'm looking forward to it

I kept it brief too, again not wanting to appear overzealous. I wondered if my message touched him or stirred up any feelings in him, the way his did for me. Probably not, I imagined. He was just a nice guy, nice to everyone. I knew this because I'd witnessed his interactions with clientele in the pub the other night. He'd probably send thoughtful, good luck messages like this one to a lot of people.

Then I thought about John and my most recent conversation with him. He had taken my advice and booked a trip to Poland to see his brother. He had so many questions about what he should pack and what he was allowed to bring in his cabin baggage etc. I couldn't escape the fact that I was probably the right person to ask, given all my flights recently. I hadn't thought too much about the luggage rules, because I'd only packed the bare minimum and was careful not to put any liquids or sharp objects into my flight bag. It wasn't rocket science but John needed reassurance nonetheless.

I also detected excitement in his voice. He thanked me for the suggestion and wondered why he didn't visit his brother more often. Michael was always inviting us over and we were always refusing. We did that a lot as a couple. We found more reasons not to do things than do them. We'd talked ourselves out of many adventures over the years.

It was only now, with a bit of distance between us, that I was analysing our relationship. I was finding holes, plenty of them. And for the first time since I'd met John, I was experiencing feelings for someone else. Not at all like the feelings I'd ever had for John. My feelings towards Phil were far different, as in they were more uncontrollable, tantalising and exciting.

Oh shit, I thought over and over—this wasn't supposed to happen. This wasn't part of my plan at all (not that I had one), but every time I tried to resist thinking about Phil, I thought of him more. His image was the last thing I pictured in my mind at night and the first thing that appeared to me in the morning. I was captivated by him. I couldn't believe these words were forming in my mind. I WAS CAPTIVATED BY HIM!

Shit...

*   *   *

I thought I'd comprehensively planned out my first morning in uni but I'd neglected to factor in the long, winding corridors, not to mention the amount of daydreaming I didn't know I'd be doing about Phil. In my daze, I got lost six times trying to find where I was supposed to be. I was showing my age, acting like an old dear who needed minding. I got concerned looks from my fellow students. They were probably wondering what this dithery, old, Irish lady was doing wandering around the grounds of the most prestigious of universities that Australia had to offer.

I figured that when I came to and banished fantasies of Phil, I'd make an effort to make some friends on campus. But his image persisted in my head and distracted me to no end.

By Wednesday I had worked myself up into a sweat about whether I should brazenly pop into the pub where I knew he'd be, or not. I really wanted to see him but feared making a fool of myself. He could have a partner or a girlfriend or a...ah, I didn't know. I didn't know and was making myself sick trying to figure it out. All I knew was that I had to find out.

I made an effort and went to the hairdressers for a much-needed trim. The hairdresser looked flabbergasted when I produced my student discount code, and then nearly fainted when she discovered it was valid. I pretended not to notice, but she clearly thought I was just chancing my arm. The discount was substantial and the trim satisfactory, so I made a further appointment to get my colour done the following week. My salt and pepper strands were starting to annoy me. I just wanted pepper.

I put on a long, flower-patterned, pink and black dress that matched my wedge sandals. I applied a little foundation and lipstick. I had a nice glow since Thailand and the air here suited me. I didn't look or feel half as washed-out as I did in Ireland. But I supposed that was down to working full time. Over here I was technically on my holidays, although that would change once my course-work piled up.

I didn't dislike my appearance in the full-length mirror and this marginal sense of satisfaction gave me just enough confidence to get as far as the door, and then down the stairs and onto the street. Although, once I set foot on the pavement I started to feel a bit doubtful. My knees were wobbling and my heart-rate increased quite suddenly. I tried to tell myself that this was my body acknowledging that I was stepping outside my comfort zone and, well, this potentially could be a good thing.

But Lord above, it was difficult. Then my feet started to feel very heavy, like they were protesting against this ridiculous journey to the pub on a Wednesday night...on my own, in an unfamiliar city, with a devoted partner back home and a nine o'clock lecture the next morning. What was I doing? I looked down at my wise feet. They spoke the truth. They were resisting the journey because they knew I was going to meet a man that I fancied and I was fifty and he might be married and *beep*— I jumped in fright as my phone beeped.

Phil
How about a brandy?

Jeepers creepers, I couldn't take these levels of excitement! My whole body shook, before hot ripples of fire burnt through me and eradicated all resistance. This was it—this was the encouragement I needed. He was inviting me for a drink. He wasn't married. He wasn't just being nice and friendly. He liked me. There WAS something there. He must have felt even a little of what I was feeling, or he wouldn't have sent that text.

I realised I was only five minutes away from the pub and it would seem highly eager to arrive so soon after his invitation, but I didn't care. I ploughed on, no longer allowing my judgemental feet to hold me back. I ignored their earlier warning signals and the more I lifted them, the less they dragged. Before I knew it, my stride turned into a determined march. I reached the pub in half the time it had previously taken me and pushed through the door.

The bubbling inferno in my gut exploded when I saw him standing at the bar. From his tall, strong frame hung a casual, grey t-shirt. I noticed his curls looked silky, like he'd just stepped out of the shower. I stuck by the door, unable to move any further, overwhelmed by the presence of this man, until he turned his head towards me. When his face lit up and he waved over, I melted. It took me a few seconds to exhale and wave back.

I lifted my stubborn, resistant feet and plodded over, not knowing what to say. I shouldn't have worried, though. He could talk for both of us.

'Hey!' he greeted me. 'You got my message?'

'Yes, but I was on my way anyway.'

He raised his brow and smiled at that. I think I even noticed him blush. Then he turned his head towards the bar and ordered a brandy for me.

'Thanks,' I said.

'No problem. Hey, d'you want to find a comfy spot and I'll bring these over?'

*   *   *

We talked, we drank and sat close to one another—closer than last week, and something had changed. The air between us had shifted. It was like I knew that he liked me, because he'd asked me out. And he knew that I liked him, because I'd admitted I was already on my way to meet him before he invited me. Our actions conveyed our feelings—his text and my march.

He reached out and touched my hand when I spoke of Callum and then I did the same when he shared the tragic story of the passing of his wife, Nicole. She died of cancer ten years ago. I squeezed his hand. I wanted to comfort him now.

I told him of Patricia's diagnosis. He asked a few questions and much to my shame, I couldn't answer most of them. It was only then I realised how shady Patricia had been of late when I asked about her treatment. She changed the subject to avoid answering and really didn't give away much. I made a mental note to ring Christy again and get a proper report from him.

I had sparkling water instead of a third brandy. I couldn't fathom the looks I'd get if the old Irish lady arrived hungover to her first lecture of the day. Phil laughed when I told him how many times I got lost in uni on Monday morning. He laughed and then told me how amazing and brave he thought I was to go to uni in a different country to follow my passion. His eyes welled up when he said it and I felt every inch of his sincerity.

When we unlocked our eyes, I said I'd better get going. He offered to walk me home. I accepted. Outside the pub, my feet were acting up again, trying to remind me of my age, my partner, my job, my studies and every other reason I shouldn't be letting this man walk me home. They went too far with their silly warnings though, and made me trip over a rise in the pavement. It led Phil to reach over and take my hand. Silly feet, I smirked to myself. *Look what you've done now!*

We walked back hand in hand the rest of the way.

Chapter Fourteen

O n reaching my apartment Phil asked if everything was okay inside and whether all the appliances were working properly.

'Yes, everything is in fine working order. I really like it too,' I reassured him.

'Well, good luck tomorrow making it to your nine o'clock lecture and not getting lost!' he joked.

I smiled back knowing this was an opportune time for a kiss goodnight. I knew he knew it too and that was why he was lingering. A knot formed in my tummy though, and I realised I hadn't told him about John. I hadn't mentioned the fact that I had a partner back home in Ireland. And I didn't want to deceive Phil in any way, or at least any more than I already had.

'Phil,' I said a little too urgently. 'I have something to tell you.' He just looked at me and didn't say anything. I continued.

'I left someone behind at home. John…his name is John, and we live together.'

'Oh,' he replied.

'I'm sorry. I should have mentioned him sooner,' I admitted.

'You left him behind? Did you not think to take him with you?' he asked with a glint in his eye.

'No,' I answered. 'I didn't want him to come. I

just wanted to get away.' That was the truth. There was a long pause. Then Phil spoke.

'I'm a little surprised,' he said. 'When I saw you weren't wearing a ring, I thought you were single.' That made the knot in my stomach even tighter. *Ouch!*

'I'm sorry I misled you. I've been thinking a lot on my travels about how much I don't miss John.' Then I paused to take a deep breath. 'And about how glad I am that he didn't come. I told him not to.' I wiped a tear from under my glasses. We were still holding hands and Phil gently squeezed mine. I squeezed back, gratefully.

'I don't want to get in the way of anything, Debra, but just know that I really like you and respect you.' With that, he released his grip and turned to walk away. I grabbed his arm.

'I really like you too, Phil. For the first time in a long time I feel excited. I'm fifty and thousands of miles from my life back home. I've realised something while I've been away. John and I were stuck in a rut. It took me leaving to realise, but I don't want to return to what we had. It wasn't special enough. I'm going to make changes, but I haven't gotten round to it yet.'

This whole conversation was making me so sad. My shoulders dropped and I started to feel deflated after all the excitement of the wonderful night I'd just had. There was more silence. Maybe he was waiting for me to finish. I looked up.

'I don't want to pass up the opportunity of

getting to know you more. The time I have here is short and...well, as I said, I'm fifty.' That made both of us smile. He took my hand again.

'Woah! Fifty! That's a pivotal age for a lot of people, right?' He grinned. 'I'm fifty-five, so I know all about it.' We giggled again. I would have put him a few years younger. His personality made him seem so.

This time I was the one who made shuffling moves to go. I turned and muttered something about my early start.

'Debra,' he said. 'I don't want to pass up this opportunity either. I appreciate you being honest with me and I trust you. I can see you're trying to figure things out. I don't know, it sounds hard, but I'll do what I can to support you.'

I looked up and met his gaze. I said thank you with my eyes. It seemed like he understood.

'I guess you've got an early start in the morning so you have to hit the sack. We had a great night. We know each other's life story now and I just have one question left.' His smile was infectious. I raised my brow, willing him to ask it.

'Can I kiss you goodnight?'

The knot in my tummy unravelled and warm ripples pulsated through my bloodstream. I grabbed his face and pulled him towards me. We kissed tenderly at first and it seemed as if he was taking my nerves into consideration. It was glorious to feel his warm, soft lips on mine and I felt the heat build when he pulled me closer. Or was it me? Did I tug him towards me? It had been a long time, or maybe never, since I'd felt this urgency to envelop someone.

Eventually, we pulled away for air. He stepped back to speak. 'Tomorrow Debs, I'll text you tomorrow, right?' I nodded, with my full heart still racing. I was both relieved and devastated that he was such a perfect gentleman and didn't try to come upstairs with me.

It took me ages to come down from the high I'd reached, but soon I fell asleep. And when I did, I slept soundly and deeply, and awoke feeling rejuvenated. I was the first to arrive for my nine o'clock lecture.

*   *   *

My morning discourse was gripping and I was so relieved that the famous Professor Cooper lived up to my expectations. I got totally engrossed in taking notes, given the subject matter was the psychology of adolescence. And when I asked a question towards the end of the lecture, we struck up a conversation. We ended up grabbing a coffee afterwards and he spoke in-depth about a student case-study he was currently working on.

He was most interested in my years of experience in teaching and career-guidance counselling and wondered if I'd have time to provide some feedback on his current project. Of course I didn't mention the tragedy that drove me to run away from my job last month, but rather embraced the chance to work with him and learn from him. I figured it would look good on my resume too.

From hearing others greet him I gathered he was known locally as Cooper, rather than Professor Cooper. He gave me his office number in case I needed anything for the course or encountered any problems. I was already excited about my next lecture with him and eager to get stuck into the case study.

I spent the rest of the afternoon in the library doing a little study. I got a text from Phil around three o'clock asking if I wanted to grab a bite to eat later. He was so casual. I loved it. No fuss, no fancy dating rituals—just a bite to eat. It suited me perfectly.

I also knew, given the extent of my feelings for Phil, that I would have to break the news to John. He would still be in Poland and I didn't want to ruin his precious time with his brother, so I planned to tell him the day he got back to Dublin. There was no easy way so I was going to be as honest as possible with him. He deserved that.

Of course, I wanted to share my newfound joy of finding Phil with Patricia. I knew she had a lot on her plate these days, but this was the type of thing she'd relish. She was never John's biggest fan in the early days, but he grew on her and she gradually accepted him as part of the family. She could plainly see how much he loved me, so that helped. But she often dropped hints that she'd prefer a more exciting partner for me, like she thought John was a little boring or something.

I rang her that night after kissing Phil goodnight. It would be early morning in Ireland, but Patricia was an early bird so I knew she'd be up. I started by asking about her health.

'I'm back at work, Deb! I took a few days to recover after my last appointment, but I couldn't wait to return to the library. It's great to be around all the kids again. Emma and Ronnie are helping out with the toddler mornings now, because that's what I find most exhausting.'

She sounded on top of the world. She loved her job and I'd heard her speak of Emma and Ronnie many times. They were by far her favourite colleagues.

'Oh Patricia, I'm so glad to hear that!' I knew if she was working she'd be happy. She loved her job at the library more than life itself.

'Well...I have some news. Can you talk, Pat? Is there anyone around?'

'Oh jeepers, this sounds interesting! Is it juicy? Christy's still in bed, don't worry. Go ahead.' Her reaction was exactly as I thought it would be. I took a deep inhale before mentioning that I'd met someone.

'What? What? You're joking, are you? No way, I don't believe you!' She roared into the phone.

'Shush! Christy will hear you. I haven't told John yet. I'll tell him when he gets home from Poland.'

'Oh my God, tell all. I want every detail. I'm boiling the kettle now. I'll need a cup of tea to calm my nerves!'

I didn't leave out any details. I described Phil's height, his frame, his clothes, his voice and his endearing grey curls to a T. I told her about the kiss and how guilty, but elated, I felt. She got so carried away with excitement that she scalded her mouth with the hot tea. Her words of encouragement were everything I wanted to hear. She told me to go for it. She said I'd never get this chance again and she wanted me to come home with no regrets.

She also agreed that John would be devastated, but promised that herself and Christy would mind him while I was away. She knew some of his friends too, so she'd make sure they checked up on him. She was beyond excited that I'd finally met someone who rocked my world—her words! She was aware that I'd never experienced this with John. We just sort of fell in with each other and got comfortable very quickly.

She knew well about these things because Christy was the love of her life and they'd always been magnetically drawn towards each other. There was nothing comfortable about their marriage. They'd been through highs and lows together, such as the worry about their daughter when she got involved in an abusive relationship and their son's addiction problems.

They'd had a rough ride, those two, but

through it all, they became closer and stronger. Everyone who knew them was in awe of their relationship and maybe even a little bit jealous. I certainly was. And I'd say John was too, though he never mentioned it.

Chapter Fifteen

After our casual dinner date, Phil walked me home and we shared another passionate kiss outside my apartment. He invited me to his place for dinner on Saturday night and I got the impression I should pack an overnight bag. He mentioned watching a movie afterwards and exact his words were, 'It might be a late night!' He winked when he said this.

I had laughed at the time but when he left and I closed the door of my apartment, I panicked. It had been so long since I'd engaged in any sort of dating experience. John and I had fallen into a routine with our sex life, which meant something usually happened once or twice a month. He was understanding of my erratic PMS, which I put down to the perimenopause.

I was just waiting now for the hot flushes to arrive, but grateful that I had Patricia's advice on reserve for when I needed it. In her words, she had "beaten" the menopause and was well-placed to be a guru of sorts in supporting me. She told me not to worry about it and promised a remedy for any and every potential symptom that I may or may not experience. Simply knowing that seemed to alleviate some of my ailments, or maybe I just felt protected by her unwavering support.

But what would happen with Phil, I

wondered. What would he expect?

The first thing I knew for sure was that I needed some new underwear. My current bra was about six years old and judging from the way everything sagged in a downward direction, I felt a bra measurement was urgently required. Before Saturday, of course. And just in case...

I had no lectures or tutorials on Friday, but I still spent the whole morning in the university library. There were a few books that Cooper had recommended and I wanted to make the most of living so close to the uni. I had no excuse not to get first class honours.

After a highly subsidised lunch at the university canteen, I dropped my books home and went bra shopping. I had to queue for twenty minutes to wait for the bra-fitting expert. I didn't even browse the lingerie while I waited, because I doubted any of the sexy stuff would suit my size. My current bra was a 38F, but it was so old and stretched that I doubted it was accurate. Therefore, I had no clue what size I should be wearing.

My bra-fitter was called Thalia and she shuddered when she saw the state of my ensemble.

'Oh my goodness, I'm so glad you came. It's time!' she bellowed in the strongest Aussie accent I'd heard since I arrived. Up to now, Phil's was.

'I know, I know. I've been a bit neglectful,' I admitted. 'Am I still a 38F?' I asked.

'No, no, in fact I doubt you were ever a 38F.

To get a good, firm support with a nice lift you're closer to a 36 triple D but...'

'Hahaha!' I laughed, remembering my nickname in secondary school. It was "Triple-D-Deb", because my full name was Debra Denise Devlin, my middle name being my late mother's given name, Denise. 'Triple D?' I repeated.

'Yeah, yeah, but I was going to say we don't actually stock triple sizes. I think maybe we'll try a 36E. You see our sizes are slightly different here to what you're used to, em, let's see...' She stood there staring at my cup size in my ill-fitting bra. I felt so exposed and old, and even a little ashamed.

Thalia was tall and slim like a model, probably a perfect 34B, I imagined. She felt the loose, over-stretched strap of my off-white bra and said, 'Hmmm, maybe we'll try a 36-double-D as well. Don't be alarmed, it's going to be a fourteen in Aussie sizes, but it should be good. I'll be back in a minute.' And off she went to find an over-the-shoulder-boulder-holder for the shabby, old, Irish lady in the changing room.

I sat down while I waited and let doubts creep in. What was I doing? Did I really want Phil to see me in a new bra? What about John? I shouldn't get too close to Phil without letting John know first. Maybe it would be a good idea to break the news to him in Poland because he'd have the support of his brother to get over the blow...

A thousand thoughts flew through my mind while I waited for Thalia. I got a fright when she returned, full of enthusiasm. 'I brought two different styles for you to try,' she said. 'This white one's hugely supportive with a bit of lift and hey, take a look at this sexy black number!' She laughed and made me laugh too. 'This is a women's victory balcony bra with a nice bit of detail on top of the cups. It's underwire too, so you'll get a great lift. So, which one do you want to try?'

'Both!' I answered immediately and we giggled.

'Good choice!' She encouraged me and I ended up buying both. Of course I did! I promised Thalia I'd dump my old bra as soon as I got home and only wear correct-fitting bras from now on. She told me that was the best news she'd heard all day and we exchanged some more banter before I left the store. I could understand how a queue had developed. She gave every customer one-hundred-percent of her attention and I imagined they all swanned off much happier than they were when they arrived. I knew I did.

*   *   *

I decided to ring John later that evening. It would be morning in Poland so he'd have the rest of the day to process what I was about to divulge. I never liked to impart bad news at night, last thing before bed. And I didn't want this task to be lingering in my mind the following night when I would be at Phil's.

John answered straight away and launched

into all of his news. This was the happiest he'd
sounded since I left him. The trip to Poland had
been good for him. Then he asked how I was.

'John, I'm good, great in fact. That's the
problem. I'm so happy over here. I don't miss home
at all.'

Silence. I expected that. He was processing.

'Michael is wondering if you'll stay over
there now that you have an apartment and your
studies. He asked if you'd left me.'

'Oh? And what did you say?'

'I said it feels like that, but I hope not. I hope
you're still coming home to me. To us, and our
house, and our life together, and your job that you
love, and your family and...'

'Okay, John.' This was going to be hard. 'The
course runs for five months, you know that, and
I've spoken to Maureen about taking a block of
unpaid leave in September. She said she'll get a sub
to cover me at school for the first term. This means
I have a bit more time to play with.'

'So you're not planning to come back? Is that
what you're trying to say?' He sounded accusatory.

'No, I will. I'll come back. I don't intend to
stay here forever. But I...I want to take a break
from us, from our relationship. If it's meant to be,
I'll come back to you, but while I'm here I want
to...' And then I stopped because I wasn't sure how
to continue.

'Ewa was right. It's a midlife crisis, that's
what she said. She thinks I should give you your

freedom and like you said, if it's meant to be...
But Deb, I already know it's meant to be. We work!
We're great for each other, everyone says so and...'

'Who says?' I asked, not that it mattered. I
didn't really care what other people thought about
us. I only knew what I felt and what I wanted. And
it wasn't John.

'I don't know—people, friends, Michael, Tom
and...'

'Okay, okay,' I interrupted. Sure, of course his
brother and friends would feel like that. I was glad
he didn't see my eye roll. I continued then. 'I want
this break, John. I want to meet other people while
I'm here. I want to make the most of my travels. I'm
not getting any younger and I don't want to pass
up any opportunities.'

'That sounds like a midlife crisis to me,' he
said in a sad tone. And then there was a few
seconds of silence.

'Maybe you're right. Maybe it is. But it's
something I have to go through and I want to do it
alone, without any ties, without you. I'm sorry,' I
said.

'Have you met someone?' It sounded as
though he already knew.

'Yes,' I admitted. Excruciating silence
ensued. I didn't know what to say. Eventually, he
spoke.

'I don't know how I feel about this, Debra. I
don't know if this is okay.'

'I understand. Take some time. Talk it

through with Michael and Ewa, I don't mind. Just try not to let it ruin the rest of your trip.'

'What about the house and...'

'John! Nothing's changing right now, okay? Don't think about any of that stuff. At least not until I come home and I WILL come home as soon as my course is finished. In the meantime, I'll ring you when you get back from Poland. We'll talk then, okay? In a few days?'

'Yeah, yeah, whatever...whatever you want,' he muttered with overwhelming resignation.

'I'm sorry, John, I...'

'Yeah, you already said that, Deb. I've got to go now. Next week...' And he hung up.

*   *   *

I told Phil everything on Saturday night. He picked me up in his Ford Transit van. We could have walked but it was cloudy with a chance of rain. He looked me up and down when I arrived downstairs to meet him.

'Looking good, Debs! Did you get your hair done?' He appeared both puzzled and impressed.

'Yes I did, thanks Phil,' I replied, failing to suppress my ear to ear beam. He'd politely mentioned my hair, but I knew it was actually my new balcony bra that made all the difference. The lift was undeniable and, personally, I found it hard to stop checking out my new cleavage at any given opportunity.

The minute I sat in his van I told him that

I'd spoken to John. I knew I probably should have waited and focussed instead on us, and our date, and his lovely car and the sights we were passing, because he seemed to know everything about the local area, but I blurted it out straight away. It hadn't left my mind.

'Oh. Is he okay?' Phil asked.

'No,' I said. 'But I think he will be. He's got family in Poland and they'll look after him. Then when he comes home, Patricia will make sure there's someone checking up on him. And he likes his job so that will keep him busy. Maybe he'll play a little more golf—he usually does when there's something on his mind. It tends to distract him.'

He turned to me. 'You okay?'

'Yes, I feel like the truth is out now and it feels good. Like a weight has been lifted. I'd been thinking about breaking up with John before I met you, y'know. Since leaving, I've discovered how much was wrong with our relationship. This would have happened anyway, just maybe not so quickly.'

No more was said. He parked underground in his urban apartment complex. He had a ground floor, two-bed that opened up onto a substantial-sized terrace. I noted the barbeque and small table with two chairs. There was a shared garden area too.

Inside I could see that he was a man of simple tastes. The walls looked freshly painted and everything was well maintained. I noticed there seemed to be a place for everything. Lots of storage, which in some ways, was the key to a woman's heart.

I smiled at him. 'I love your apartment, Phil. It's so bright and airy.'

He seemed as delighted as I'd been when he complimented my haircut. 'Yeah, I moved here about six years ago and brightened up the colour of the walls. I built a few extra presses for all my tools and that. Can't have plungers and hammers lying around now, can I?' We giggled.

'Well I think it looks great!'

'Thanks, Debs. Hungry?' he asked.

'Are you cooking?' I wondered if he was planning to order in.

'I could throw a few shrimp on the barbie,' he winked when he said that.

'Hahaha! Anything, Phil,' I smiled and he got to work.

He had delicate, ready-made, shrimp skewers that he took out of the fridge. He also removed a large bowl of chopped peppers, aubergine and onion. He wrapped the veg in tinfoil and added seasoning, a dash of oil and some sauce.

'This is going on the barbie too,' he informed me. He seemed to know what he was doing. I sat down, tried to relax and picked up the newspaper I'd spotted on a shelf by the table.

'Oh sorry, Debs. I never even offered you a drink. You can tell I'm out of practice with this kinda stuff.' Was he? Was he really? A handsome guy like him...out of practice? I found that hard to believe. He went and fetched a bottle of chardonnay from the fridge and I nodded.

'That would be lovely, thanks. Can I help with anything?'

'Nah, nah, you just sit there and look pretty.' I raised my eyes and shook my head, but couldn't help tittering.

The chardonnay was crisp and refreshing. The shrimp was a little hard to eat off the skewer, but we just laughed at each other's attempts, before competing to see who could make the bigger mess of it. The veg was like a rainbow of colour and he had some fresh bread that he'd just picked up from the bakery next door. I couldn't remember ever having such a delicious meal, and in such delightful company too.

I really felt like I was on my holidays with this glorious Aussie man, enjoying this delicious Aussie meal. Even though it was winter in Sydney, I felt so far removed from cloudy Dublin. And when the rain came and we moved inside, it felt like a different kind of rain, more exotic than the dreary drops back home.

After dinner we had some ice cream and moved to the couch, where he showed me his vast DVD collection. He liked physical media and hadn't exactly moved with the times when it came to streaming. But I kind of admired his old-fashioned nature and sentimentality. We talked about some of the movies in his collection, but I had no desire to watch one.

I went to the bathroom and when I came back, Phil had turned on some music.

'That's beautiful,' I said. 'What is it?'

'Villagers. I thought you might know them? They're from Ireland.'

'Oh, I don't tend to keep up...'

'Yeah, I can't listen to any of the music I used to like, because it reminds me of Nicole. I boxed up our shared CD's and gave them to a charity shop. But eh... I love listening to music, so I made it my mission to find some modern stuff that I love and won't have any connections with her. Y'know, my music for my new life.' He looked at me with a pained expression, but I think I detected hope in his eyes.

I sat down beside him. 'Well...I love it, Phil. You've found something special.' He looked at me and we kissed, with the sweet sound of 'Dawning On Me' by Villagers playing in the background. I heard every word of the song and felt each and every one of them.

Chapter Sixteen

A s it turned out, Phil seemed to share my lack of interest in watching a movie. We kissed on the couch until the song ended. Then he offered me another drink and I said no. We looked at each other. In my mind it was obvious what I wanted. I didn't think words were required. He reached out his hand to help me up and I took it. He led me to the bedroom and as soon as we entered, he turned to me. 'Are you sure about this, Debs?'

I didn't hesitate. 'Never been surer!' I smiled, like I nearly always did in his company. How did I find this man, or did he find me? He was everything I'd ever wanted, even though I never knew it until I met him. There was nothing about him so far that I didn't absolutely love.

His height, his frame, his strength, his hair, his eyes, his smile, his van, his apartment, his shrimp...heck, the list was endless. I loved everything, but it was mainly his larger-than-life personality that had won me over. He was so friendly, easygoing and casual, yet thoughtful and sensitive. He was funny and cheeky and I'd bet money on it that he'd been a bad boy in his youth.

But life had changed him and taught him lessons and now he came across as a generous, open-hearted soul. I just felt so lucky to have stumbled across him, and even luckier that he seemed to like me too. I thought of him welling up when he told me he was impressed with what I was doing in uni, and how he'd said I was brave. His support meant so much to me and, despite being thousands of miles from home, I'd met someone that made me feel like I WAS home.

*   *   *

He had problems with my new bra. When I tried to help, I made things worse. Then I had problems with my new bra. I had to tell him it was a new bra. He made lots of "woohoo" noises and wolf whistles, which had both of us in hysterics. It wasn't opening, though. I told him to cut it. He asked me how much I'd paid for it and when I told him it was seventy dollars, he refused to cut it. He turned me over on my tummy and fiddled with it for a good five minutes before songs of victory bellowed from his mouth.

He whipped the bra off once it came undone and danced around the bedroom, singing 'We Are The Champions' by Queen. Then he inserted a CD into his ancient-looking CD player and blasted 'Ain't No Stoppin Us Now'. For this number, he boogied with my new bra as his dance partner, lip synching all the way. I sat there, topless on his bed, screaming with laughter.

When the song ended, he flung the bra over his shoulder and dived onto the bed. He grabbed my triple D breasts and we kissed as if we'd only just discovered the art of kissing and needed to show the world how it was done. We made love, and the moment we finished we kissed tenderly, like how I'd always imagined it was meant to be. He grabbed the remote before I could stop him and blared 'Ain't No Stoppin Us Now' once again.

I pulled him to me and whispered so close to his ear that I could feel my lips brushing off his lobes—'You make me so happy, Phil.'

'Ditto Debs,' he replied and like immature teenagers, we giggled at the alliteration. The next few weeks in Sydney were filled with love-making, smiling until my cheeks hurt and intense affection. I was definitely falling for him and he made it clear he was falling for me too, especially when he shared his plans with me.

*   *   *

It was a Saturday night and he'd booked a restaurant in the city. We got a taxi, even though I let him know the train would be far more cost-effective. But he insisted, and said it was his treat. He also mentioned he had something to ask me.

With other men or in other relationships and given the intensity of ours, one might assume that this could be a marriage proposal. But this was Phil. And, although I knew it would be something great, I figured it would also be unconventional and unexpected. He just had an innate sensibility to surprise me with something quirky each time we met.

It wasn't just any restaurant he brought me

to. It was a fine dining, award-winning restaurant in the central business district. I gave out to him about the fact that he didn't warn me it was going to be so fancy, but he insisted, like he always did, that I looked "great".

I ordered food I'd never before sampled and everything was mouth-watering and morish. My Murray cod masgouf served with double apple and ajwain was to die for, and we both got drunk on cocktails. Eventually, he shared his proposal.

'Debs, you know how I've mentioned I take off every year for a few weeks? Well...I've been saving up for a trip of a lifetime. It was something Nicole and I had briefly discussed, but she wanted kids so that took over from any travel plans. It wasn't long after our many failed attempts that we found out she had cancer. That put an end to both our family plans and our travel plans.' I reached out and held his hand.

'It's okay. I've come to terms with not having a family and being a father, but I haven't forgotten about my travel dreams. I put them on hold while I sold our house in the suburbs. Y'know too many memories of Nicole to stay there, so I had to sell up. I moved back to Sydney where I grew up so that I could be near my mates and family.'

'But why are you telling me this?' I was confused. He was going into a lot of detail and I'd just had three very strong cocktails.

'I'm telling you this because after I bought my apartment and quit my old job and that, I was a little strapped for cash, but I worked hard and put my money towards a travel fund. I figure that's something I can still do now on my own, and I think Nicole would give me her blessing if she could.'

'Oh,' I said, as my heart hit the floor. He was going away. I'd just met the man of my dreams and he was planning to leave.

'Yeah, my dream is to go to Bali and stay for a few months, before heading further afield. Usually, I head away for a few weeks, but I've saved enough now to make this one a big one. And I've wrangled the time off work too. I want to go river rafting in Bali, check out the waterfalls and absorb all that the country has to offer. I'm even game to meditate with the monks, see the temples and go trekking.' He paused, and I admired the child-like excitement in his expression. He inhaled and continued. 'So…what d'you say, Debs? Are you game?'

'Excuse me? Sorry?' Did I hear him correctly? Was he asking if I was game to go trekking in waterfalls and meditate with monks? The cocktails really had gone to my head.

'Nah, nah, I mean like when you finish your studies, like in December? I've booked six months off work. It means doing a hell of a lot of overtime and working weekends between now and then, but it's a dream of a lifetime so it'll be worth it. My mates know I've been planning this for years. I always thought I'd go on my own but now that I've met you, I was thinking, maybe...you'd come with me? Even join me for a little while? What d'you think?'

In that instant all the changes in my life in the last few months flashed before my eyes. How I had gone further and further from my comfort zone in such a short space of time and not only survived, but thrived. I looked into Phil's hopeful eyes and felt nothing but unconditional, unfaltering love towards him.

'Yes!' I exclaimed. 'Yes, I'll go with you.' We kissed and downed the rest of our cocktails. We got a taxi back to his place and made love. The next morning he took me to meet his brother and his wife and their family. It was a beautiful day. I loved them and they seemed to like me. We arranged to meet them the following week at a festival in Sydney.

Luck was on my side with my studio apartment too. Marcus was offered a tutoring position in the US and wouldn't be returning until Christmas. He was happy with our arrangement. Phil even took photos of the apartment to reassure Marcus of how well I was looking after it.

I had assignments to complete in the following few days so I didn't see Phil, although we spoke and texted. I hadn't heard much from John in recent weeks, but Patricia had been keeping in touch with him and texted me to let me know he was coping on his own.

I thought about Patricia and how she kept

missing my calls recently. On each occasion she'd text me back with an apology and a valid reason why she'd missed my call, yet she didn't ring me back. I was dying to tell her of my plans to go travelling with Phil. I'd built it up in my head that it would be a trip of a lifetime, but she never picked up when I called. It was too important and thrilling to share in a text. I wanted to tell her in person and hear her reaction.

After a crazy amount of unanswered calls, I eventually decided to ring her husband, Christy. He hadn't returned my calls either in recent weeks, but he was a workaholic so I understood and forgave him. I'd always had an amazing relationship with Christy. I loved how he loved Patricia so completely and respected how close we were as sisters. He'd always take a step back if we needed each other for any reason.

I was so relieved when he finally answered my call this time. But then I wasn't sure...was it the naive excitement in my voice that broke him?

All I knew was, I asked if there was something wrong with Patricia's phone because she hadn't answered my calls in two weeks and he went dead silent. That unnerved me. Christy and I had always enjoyed easy conversation. We were never stuck for words.

'Christy? Christy, what's wrong?' I pleaded. 'What is it?' After a long pause, he spoke.

'Debra, it's Patricia,' he said. 'I think you should come home.'

Chapter Seventeen

I dropped the phone and accidentally hung up. What did he mean? What was he trying to tell me? I rang back immediately.

'Christy, what's going on? Please tell me now!'

'Debra, I shouldn't be telling you this. She made me swear not to, but I think I'll regret it if I don't.'

'Oh God, what is it, Christy? You have to tell me!' My heart was pounding so fast it pained me.

'She's been avoiding talking to you because the cancer has spread. It's in her throat now and she doesn't sound the same. You'd know straight away if you heard her. And…she doesn't want you to know because she doesn't want you to come home.'

'What? What? I still don't understand. Is she in the hospital?' Confusion, panic and fear engulfed me. The throbbing spread to my head and I had to hold onto my glasses for fear they'd get knocked off.

'She knows you're having the time of your life out there and she's proud of you getting your psychology qualification and…'

'Christy, stop! Cut to the chase!' I knew he was dancing around the real issue.

'We got bad news, Debra, very bad news. It's

terminal, a matter of weeks, the doctor said.' He broke down. I heard him weep. I'd never heard Christy get emotional like this before.

'Weeks? Weeks? Are you serious? I don't understand. She told me she was back at work and I thought she was getting better!'

'She went back a couple of mornings here and there, against doctor's orders. She was supposed to be resting, but you know Patricia. I couldn't stop her. She loves her job and...' I could hear him sobbing.

'So then she lied to me about getting better? I don't believe it. If I'd known I would have come home and...'

'Debra, Debra, don't you see? That's exactly what she doesn't want. She wants you to stay and she's even left orders for you not to return for the funeral. I'm going against her wishes by telling you all of this, but I think it's the right thing to do. I'm sorry, Debra, I don't know what to say or do anymore. This is, this is just...' He choked up again and my heart broke for him.

Christy was always the strong one holding everything together, and now he couldn't speak through his tears. I thanked him for being honest with me and told him I would see him soon. I also told him he needn't say anything to Patricia about our phone call, but I would be back to see her soon.

I didn't hesitate about going against Patricia's wishes. I wanted to be by her side. I just had a few things to do first. I couldn't even imagine what I would say to Phil, so I put him to the bottom of my list for now. The first thing I did was make an appointment with Cooper at uni.

*   *   *

He was so understanding. He would do everything he could to help me transfer my course back to UCND in Dublin. He was a family man and the minute I told him about Patricia he promised to handle the admin, so I could transition smoothly. He reassured me that any assignments done to date wouldn't be lost.

The next person I rang was John. He knew, of course he knew, but he'd been sworn to secrecy too.

'I wanted to tell you, Deb, but Pat and Christy made me promise. We didn't want to go against her wishes, but I'm glad you know now. It's only right what Christy did.'

'I'm still in shock about the whole thing, John. But I know how strong-willed Patricia is so I think I understand why you were afraid to tell me,' I said, even though I was raging to have been left out of the loop. I didn't want them feeling worse than they already did. And anyway, this wasn't about me. It was about Patricia.

'Are you coming home, Deb?' He sounded hopeful.

'Of course, John, of course I am. She's dying. Of course I'm coming home to be with her.'

'Yeah. I'm glad you're coming. I'll pick you

up. You just let me know when you book your flight, okay Deb?' He was so kind it brought tears to my eyes.

'Okay John, I will, thanks.' When I hung up I broke into tears. I'd hurt John so much in recent months, yet he was still there for me. He was there for Patricia and Christy too. He was family. And here I was on the other side of the world living my best life while all my loved ones were suffering at home.

That familiar feeling of guilt I'd experienced after Callum's passing returned. It deflated me entirely. It reduced me to stone. I didn't do anything for a few days, apart from attending uni. I spent the rest of the time sprawled on the couch or taking painkillers to help me sleep. I fobbed off Phil's texts by lying that I was studying for a test. I told him I'd see him at the weekend.

I didn't even have the wherewithal to book my flight home. Every time I tried I encountered a problem, like not having enough time to make a connecting flight or having to stay overnight in Dubai. With each new search a new obstacle would appear. Why couldn't I do this? I gave up and berated myself, before crumbling on the couch.

And it wasn't just about my dying sister. It was about Callum, and his family, and my students and how I'd run away from things at school. It was about John too. I felt bad for how I'd treated him, as if our ten years together meant nothing to me. I'd have to find a way to make it up to him.

And Phil—every time I thought about him and what this would do to our budding relationship, I cried. Things had been looking bright for us, especially with me agreeing to go travelling with him. I knew he'd had other relationships since Nicole died. I wasn't the first and probably wouldn't be the last. A handsome, beautiful man like him wouldn't be without female company for too long.

I reassured myself that he'd been planning this trip long before he met me and always intended to go alone. I just knew I didn't want our relationship to end so soon, but how could it work out now? There was only one thing to do. I texted him to come over to my apartment on Friday evening as soon as he finished work. I needed to speak to him before I booked any flights or did anything official. I needed to tell him everything and, more than anything, I needed a hug from him.

*　　*　　*

He arrived grinning, bearing a bunch of flowers. He looked fresh, clean and just out of the shower. The ends of his curls were still wet. With his one free arm he grabbed me and kissed me and said he'd missed me. I took the flowers from him and when he came inside he looked at me properly and immediately asked what was wrong.

I looked towards him with tears welling up in my eyes already. 'I think you're going to need to sit down for this, Phil,' I said.

'Ah no, sweetheart, what is it? What's wrong?' He put his arm around me and we sat on the tiny couch.

'It's my sister,' I said. 'Patricia's cancer is terminal. She only has a few weeks,' I managed before breaking down.

'Ah no! I know how close you two are. There's not a day gone by since we met that you haven't mentioned her name. Come here.' He pulled me closer and stroked my back.

I took a tissue out of my pocket and blew my nose until I felt ready to speak again.

'Phil, I'm so sorry to be sharing this with you. It must bring back memories of Nicole. I understand if you need to go. This must be triggering for you...'

'Debs, Debs, no, I'd rather be here for you. I've had countless therapy sessions since Nicky passed and I've come to terms with it. I mean, I miss her every day, but I accept that she's gone and not coming back. And I guess I know she'd want me to be happy. Somehow that makes it easier to accept. It's okay, you can share your feelings about Patricia with me.'

I kissed him on the lips. He was saying all the right things.

'I can't stay here in Sydney, Phil. I have to go home and be with her. I'm sorry this is all so sudden.' I didn't know what else to say.

'It's out of your control, I understand. You

have to be with Patricia, but how come you only found out now? Surely, she's known for a while? Nicky found out she was terminal when she still had six months left.'

'Yeah, well, that's a bone of contention now. She's been hiding it from me on purpose. In fact, it sounds like she's been hiding the truth from everyone. She doesn't want anyone to worry. She even went into work last week against doctor's orders. She's very strong-willed.'

'You two are alike, then?' Phil smiled.

'I suppose,' I sighed and smiled back. He had a point. 'But she really didn't want me to find out. She wanted me to get my qualification here in Sydney and she knew how happy I was here. She knew I'd met you and didn't want to jeopardise my time here. She's that type of person, just wanting everyone else to be happy. She cares more for others than for herself.'

'She sounds incredible.' He took my hand and squeezed it.

'She doesn't know I know, y'know.'

'What's that now?' He looked baffled. I couldn't help smiling briefly.

'She doesn't know that I found out she's terminal. Her husband, Christy, told me even though she made him promise he wouldn't. I'm just going to pretend I'm doing project work for my course and say that I booked a trip home to surprise everyone. I don't want Christy getting into trouble for being honest with me.'

'Yeah, yeah, good plan. Don't land him in it. Don't shoot the messenger and all that...' He leaned back on the couch.

'Oh sorry, Phil, you must be starving. You didn't get dinner after work, did you? Let me fix you something.'

'No, no, you've just gotten this terrible news. Sit down. I'll order in.'

I accepted. We shared a takeaway curry and I broached the subject of our relationship.

'You know, I'm only going home for a few months. I plan to come back. I don't want to break up with you or anything. You make me so happy and I hate to leave.'

'I know. All my mates are asking what my secret is. They want to know what's putting the big, goofy smile on my face lately. I've told them about you. We were onto a good thing, you and me, Debs.' We locked eyes and smiled.

'We sure were. I don't want it to end.' I looked down. 'But I have to go. And I can't say how long I'll be. I just don't know.'

'Say no more. Don't stress yourself out. I, of all people, understand what you're going through. You have to go and be there for Patricia. It takes as long as it takes. We'll stay in touch. You can't get rid of me that easily, y'know.'

'What about the apartment? I hate to let Marcus down. Is there anything I can do?'

'Ah, don't worry about him. Hey, maybe you could advertise the place on the noticeboard in uni? I'm sure someone would jump at the chance. I know Marcus didn't want students in here, but I'll vet them first and keep an eye on the place for him. We'll get that sorted.'

'Okay then, I'll go to uni on Monday to tie up loose ends. I was thinking of booking a midweek flight. I'd better do that sooner rather than later and see what's available.'

'Want any help with that? Why don't you get your laptop? Booking flights is a headache. Let's do it together while I'm here.'

He was right. His help was invaluable. I probably would have ended up back in Bangkok had it been left to me. My brain was all over the place. I'd be leaving on Tuesday. Phil said he'd take the afternoon off work to bring me to the airport.

*   *   *

Phil's last words or near last words to me stuck in my head and brought a warm, fuzzy feeling to my insides—

'We won't get mushy at the airport, right Debs? This isn't goodbye. It's a thank you for sharing the last few months with me. It's been a blast! And you're a top, mature, Irish lady, you know that?'

All I could think about on my long flight home was that old Alfred Tennyson quote—*'Tis better to have loved and lost than never to have loved at all.*

Chapter Eighteen

I cried and slept in equal amounts on the way back to Dublin. All of my loved-up glow from meeting Phil and my sun kissed skin had faded with the tears I shed. The skin around my eyes was dry and scaly due to the copious amount of tissues employed to wipe them. I'd say I looked as though I'd aged about twenty years from the flight alone.

But when I landed in Dublin a profound, laid-back, calm feeling descended upon me as passport security waved me on with a nod and a smile. I obviously didn't pose a threat.

I wasn't aware that I'd missed Ireland until I returned. Now that I was back it felt like I was home, as if this was where I was supposed to be. It was both comforting and worrying as I wondered if I'd ever have the impetus to travel again.

I was fumbling for my phone to call a taxi at arrivals when I heard my name. I looked up.

'John! What are you doing here?' I was gobsmacked.

'You texted me your flight details. Don't you remember? Deb, you look amazing, it's so good to see you!' I laughed because I knew I didn't look amazing at all. I was exhausted and puffy-eyed from crying, but it had been a while so maybe he thought I'd left in a worse state than the one I was currently in. I looked at John. Gone was the old, worn, brown jacket and he seemed younger, healthier and in far better shape than when I left. I wasn't expecting that.

He reached out to hug me and welcome me home. 'You look great, John,' I said and I meant it. 'Have you been working out or something?'

He laughed. 'Well, I did a little manual labour in Poland to help Michael and pulled something in my back. I ended up going to physio when I got home and the exercises really helped. He also recommended swimming so I joined the gym on MacMillan Road and I started swimming twice a week.' He seemed thoroughly chuffed with himself.

'Wow! That's amazing! You look far healthier than when I left!' I beamed, but he looked down. 'Well, looks can be deceptive, Deb. I've missed you,' he said and then reached out to pull me to him again. I let him hold me for a minute. It was cathartic.

When I pulled away I got straight to the point. 'Have you seen Patricia?'

'I saw her last week. I'm one of the few people in the loop. She hasn't even come clean to her work colleagues at the library.'

'Oh. Does she know I came home?'

'No. I haven't said anything and neither has Christy. Nobody else knows you're coming, unless you told someone?'

'No, not a soul,' I said. 'Though, I must get in touch with Maureen soon, and I think I'll ring

Mae later. Thanks, John.' I squeezed his arm and he drove me home.

It all felt so natural. We chatted non-stop in the car and he boasted about how well he'd taken care of the house and the plants. He'd also kept in touch with our mutual friends, even though it wasn't easy. I was impressed with how well he'd held it together. I pondered that maybe I'd never really challenged him before.

When I walked through the front door, I felt a huge rush of love and familiarity for our little house. John had taken care of it. I couldn't remember ever seeing it look so immaculate.

He excitedly showed me what he'd painted, which hinges he'd oiled and the cupboard doors he'd fixed. Then I was blown away when he took me upstairs. He'd cleared out all the junk from the spare room and stored most of it up in the attic. He'd turned the space into a beautiful, functional second bedroom. I noticed his clothes in the wardrobe and his pyjamas folded on the bed.

'Have you been sleeping here, John?' I asked. It was much smaller than our double room next door.

'Up to now, no, but I moved my stuff in so I'll stay in here now that you're home. I thought you'd like to be back in your own bed and have some space to settle in.'

I was flabbergasted. Such forward thinking on his part. I hadn't even considered the sleeping arrangements on my return.

'John, have you been seeing a therapist or something?' This seemed like the advice of an expert to me.

'Yes, it was Ewa's idea. She said to check with work and see if they offered subsidised mental-health counselling. Most state jobs do nowadays. I checked it out and got five free sessions. If I want or need more, I'll have to pay from now on.'

'Wow, John, this is so unlike you. I'm genuinely impressed and good on Ewa for thinking of that!' We smiled at each other and he relished the praise I lavished upon him. 'Right, I need to get showered and changed and then you can take me to Patricia.' I made to walk out of the room, but jumped in fright when he barked in response, 'No!'

I stopped and turned around. 'What d'you mean? This is why I came home. I came to see Patrica!' He looked very hurt when I said this. I should have thought to be more sensitive and said I'd come to see him too, but the truth was I hadn't.

'The hospice is very strict. You wouldn't be allowed in now.'

'The hospice? What hospice? Isn't she at home?'

'No. I'm sorry, Debra. She's seeing out her days in the hospice in Murphy's Square. You'll have to make an appointment to see her. They're very rigid with their visiting hours.'

'What? But I'm her sister and I've just flown from the other side of the world to see her!'

'They won't care, Debra. People are dying there. Even Christy has to let them know when he's coming and no visitors are allowed after seven.' I looked at the clock. It was twenty past seven. I sat down on the bed. He sat beside me and patted my back.

'There's some salad in the fridge. Will I fix you a sandwich and you can have an early night? You must be exhausted after the flight.'

I took a few deep breaths. He was right. I was. I accepted his offer and went to bed at nine. I got changed and lay down on my old bed...our old bed. It was much more comfortable than the firm mattress I'd slept on in Sydney.

I was home. It was blissful and peaceful. And I slept soundly.

*   *   *

John had taken the day off work so he could bring me to the hospice. I rang first thing and they said she'd slept well and I could come to visit at ten o'clock. I felt awful that I had nothing to bring to her, but John said she wouldn't want anything anyway. He told me she was being fed via a tube at the moment because her throat was so painful.

All of this new information made me feel like an extremely bad sister, off following my dreams in Oz when my best friend, sister and confidante was suffering so direly at home. We drove in silence because I was dying inside, and John knew it. He also knew what was ahead of me in the hospice, as he'd been in with her recently.

I checked in and was immediately led to her room. I saw colourful, hand-drawn pictures on the cork board beside her door, no doubt crafted by the kids she worked with in the library. The nurse knocked gently and tipped open her door.

'Patricia,' she whispered. 'You have a visitor, and it's not Christy!' she joked.

Patricia was lying down and lifted her head slightly to see who the mysterious visitor was.

'Debra!' she croaked. 'Oh my God, Debra!' She raised two hands for me to come and hug her. I did and as soon as I felt her limp embrace, I broke down in her arms. She patted me on the back to comfort me.

'What did you come home for?' she whispered.

'I came to see you.' I hugged her tighter.

'I wanted you to stay in Oz and be a student again with Phil. I'm grand here. I've everything I want and need. Who told you? Did Christy tell you to come? Or was it John?'

'Neither. I transferred my postgrad back to Dublin to do a project. I surprised John and rang your house to let you know I was home. That was when Christy told me you weren't at home at all. You were here. I wish you'd told me, though. I was under the impression you were in remission. I wish you'd told me the truth.'

'Deb, I'm dying, and you being here isn't going to change that. Christy is suffering enough along with me, and both Daniel and Amy are here. They've been great. They're all looking after me and crying with me. I want for nothing, Deb, honestly. You go back now, back to Phil in Sydney. I hope you didn't break up with him, did you?'

'No.' I decided I'd just tell her whatever made her happy. She had to whisper as her voice was gravelly. It was probably a huge effort for her to even talk. 'No, we're keeping in touch,' I smiled. 'I'm so glad Daniel and Amy are here to support you.' Patricia didn't see enough of her two children since they moved out in their early twenties. 'Is Daniel staying with Christy?'

'Yeah, he's delighted. And so am I. He's not on his own,' she smiled, but I noticed her bright blue eyes welling up.

'Yes, that's great. And now you've one more person to cry with and suffer with, because I'm putting everything on hold to be here for you and spend time with you.' She pulled me nearer.

'Thanks, Deb. I love you. It's so good to see you.' That set both of us off. This was going to be an emotional few weeks.

The nurse came in after an hour and a half with medications for Pat. She asked me to make another appointment at reception to come back and visit. I did that and texted John. He was in the coffee shop. The minute he saw my tear-soaked eyes, he said—'Christy now? Will I take you to Christy's?'

I had to see my brother-in-law to hug him

and thank him for looking after Pat so well. She seemed to have made peace with the fact that she was dying, but that must be hard for Christy to accept.

My nephew, Daniel, answered the door and exclaimed, 'Auntie Debra!' He gave me a warm, bear hug. I hadn't seen him in five years, since he left for the States and didn't come back. My next bear hug came from Christy and I cried on his shoulder.

'How did she take it, Debra? I said nothing. I didn't tell her you were coming.'

'Well, she was delighted to see me at first,' I said. 'And then she told me to go back to Oz because she has everything she needs.'

'Oh no!' he replied. 'Only Pat would say that!'

'Where's Amy?' I asked, because I couldn't wait to embrace my niece.

'At home with the kids. They'll come and stay for the weekend, so she'll be here tomorrow. Here, sit down. I'll put the kettle on.' I looked at John to check if that was okay with him and he nodded.

It seemed like he'd been spending a lot of time with Christy and Patricia since I left. My family, I thought, all looking after each other in my absence. My family—I secretly smiled at the comforting thought of them. John caught my eye and smiled too, as if reading my thoughts.

Chapter Nineteen

We ended up staying for dinner. Daniel went in to see Patricia in the afternoon and Christy did the evening visit. He said he always liked to see her at the end of the day so he could kiss her goodnight. My heart melted when he shared stuff like that and I wondered how he would ever cope without her.

I couldn't believe that she'd forced Christy to bring her into work during the week. A few days before I got home, she'd made Christy take her into the library for one last toddler storytime. He almost had to kidnap her from the hospice as the staff were very disapproving, but Patricia got the final say.

Christy said he got a wheelchair from the ward and a warm blanket for her lap. With all eyes on her, he wheeled her into the storytime session. He delighted in sharing their adventure with us—

'She wanted to see her friend, Emma, deliver the story to the toddlers one last time. She got plenty of hugs from the kids, and their parents squeezed her hand in gratitude. She couldn't talk to anyone as her throat was particularly bad that day, but she managed to howl with laughter along with the toddlers in response to Emma's story.'

It warmed our hearts to hear how much she enjoyed what ended up being her last outing.

'I spoke to her colleague, Ronnie, who was amazed to see her. I told him she threatened to haunt me from the afterlife if I refused to bring her!' We all laughed in agreement—that was so Patricia!

John drove me home and we talked about Patricia's crazy antics over the years. He was very fond of her and was going to miss her almost as much as me. When we got home he made tea and we sat on the couch.

'Movie?' he offered, thinking it would help get my mind off the hospice and Patricia. Unfortunately for him, it only served to trigger thoughts of Phil, as I remembered the night I went to his apartment to watch a movie and we didn't last long on the couch. I turned to John.

'Thanks, but no. I think I'll go and read some of my course notes online. But thanks for carting me around today. I'm not sure if I could have driven through the tears. I appreciate you being here for me, John. I don't expect it after the way I've treated you.'

'Let's park all that for now, Debra. We'll focus on Patricia for the time being. Between my work, your studies and, of course, my new exercise regime, we've enough to keep us occupied. We'll have plenty of time to talk about us in the long run.' He smiled before leaning over to kiss me on the cheek. Then he picked up the cups and went to wash them.

I went into the livingroom and while I

waited for my laptop to fire up, I thought about John and how he'd changed. He didn't seem as resigned or apathetic as he was before I left. It seemed to me that the trip to Poland and his rigorous fitness routine had given him a new lease of life. He was much more upbeat and was saying and doing all the right things.

He wasn't putting any pressure on me. I liked the way he'd vacated our bedroom to give me space to settle back in. I needed it. I knew I hadn't wanted to sleep with him on my return, so this gave me time to figure things out.

I'd received a couple of texts from Phil asking if I was okay. I told him that John had picked me up from the airport, but I hoped he didn't automatically think we were getting back together. His texts were brief and so were mine. I had it in my head to arrange a call with him as soon as I'd settled in. I decided to write it down on my to-do list. I missed his gregarious personality, even though I couldn't see how it would fit into my life here in Dublin. I looked forward to hearing his voice on the phone nonetheless.

*   *   *

My first week with Patricia was filled with me going to the hospice every day and fulfilling any requests she had. And she had plenty! I made lists, as many of her wishes needed to be carried out posthumously. We giggled about some of it despite the morbidity of it all. She could still make me laugh, even in her suffering.

I left her on Thursday morning with her asking me why I hadn't spoken to Phil yet. He hadn't called me, but maybe he was thinking I was back with John since we were cohabiting. I texted him to check if he wanted to talk. His texts of late were always brief. 'You bet!' he texted back.

In the afternoon while John was at work, I gave him a call.

'Hey Debs! So good to hear your voice! So tell me, how is she? Did she get a surprise when she saw you?'

'Haha, yes! She actually gave out to me and told me to go back to Oz, but no, she was delighted to see me. I've seen her every day since and I wish I could say she was improving, but she seems to be getting weaker by the day.'

'Ah no, that must be hard. I bet you're glad you went home, though?'

'Absolutely! It was the right thing to do. Not even just for Patricia, but for the family too. It's been so hard on all of them.'

'Yeah, it's a tough time. I remember it well.'

'And how have you been, Phil?' I didn't say I missed him, because with everything going on I hadn't time to miss him. And I didn't want to just say it for the sake of it.

'Busy, keeping busy, I guess. I've already leased the apartment. Another mature student, so Marcus is happy.'

'Oh wow, that was quick! That's great. I felt

bad about leaving so abruptly.'

'No, no, like you said, it was the right thing to do.' A short pause followed before I spoke.

'Emm, Phil, I'm not sure why I'm telling you this, but although John and I are living together, we're actually in separate bedrooms. He had it all arranged and wanted to give me space to settle in. I don't know, I suppose I just wanted to let you know that even though he's being supportive, we're not back together or anything.'

'Oh, I see. I did wonder actually, but I didn't want to intrude. I know your family comes first, so I guess I was waiting for you to call me.'

That little exchange seemed to break the ice and we carried on chatting for almost an hour. It was late in Sydney and he had to get to bed as he had an early start in the morning. Before saying goodbye, he asked if he could call again soon and I told him I'd love that. When we ended our phone call, to my horror, I realised I had three missed calls from Christy and two from Daniel. My heart plummeted and my hand started to shake.

That was when I heard the front door. 'Debra? Debra, are you here?' John shouted.

'Yes,' I called back. 'I'm in the living room, John.'

'Have you heard? I got a call from Christy while I was at work.'

'No,' I said, hand still trembling. 'Heard what?'

'Patricia's taken a turn for the worse. Close

family members can come and stay by her bedside. Are you ready to go? I'll drive.'

'Oh God, no! They said a few weeks...she has a few weeks left. This is too soon, John. This can't be happening.' But John was dashing around getting things like snacks, my coat and my glasses case. 'C'mon Debra, let's go.'

*　　*　　*

When we arrived Amy almost fell at my feet. She was so delighted to see me, but an absolute emotional wreck. She had featured in many of Patricia's posthumous requests. Patricia had warned that she'd need a lot of looking after. I picked her up and we embraced. We linked arms as we made our way to Patricia's room.

John waited outside, as only Christy, Daniel, Amy and I were admitted. Christy hugged me immediately when he saw me. 'She's unresponsive, Deb,' he said, eyes wide with panic and exhaustion.

'I saw her this morning, Christy, and she was in good form. Notably weak, but we were able to have a conversation.'

'Yeah, Daniel was with her this afternoon and she was okay for a while and then got very tired. She fell asleep earlier than usual and when her breathing slowed down, they rang me. They told me it's a matter of days, or maybe even hours. They can't tell for sure, but I get the feeling the end is near,' he whispered the last part to protect Patricia, just in case she could hear us.

We all took turns holding her hand and whispering sweet nothings in her ear. Daniel had done some research and discovered that towards the end of life, hearing was the last sense to go. He played her favourite songs on repeat on his phone, hoping it would trigger some movement or recognition in his mother.

It was then I understood what Phil meant about not being able to listen to the music he shared with Nicole. I didn't think I'd ever listen to Elton John or Fleetwood Mac again after this. It would be too triggering and I wouldn't want reminders of these fear-filled hours.

I told John to go home. He came in briefly, squeezed Patricia's hand and whispered an emotional goodbye to her. I hugged him tightly. Neither of us wanted to let go but he eventually did. Then he promised to come back first thing in the morning.

The four of us stayed chatting and humming along to the music all night. The staff brought tea and sandwiches for us and made sure Patricia was comfortable.

She looked content and happy, as if midway through a dream and enjoying a sound night's sleep. That was why I simply couldn't believe that she passed away at eleven minutes past six that morning. I couldn't believe she had died like that. I could have sworn she was just sleeping.

Chapter Twenty

T he next few days were hazy, but a few memories stood out. The funeral was as cheerful as it was poignant, especially when Daniel delivered the eulogy. The phrase "life and soul of the party" stood out, and he captured his mother's exuberance in his ten minute speech.

As we exited the church behind the coffin, ripples of laughter echoed throughout when the song 'Always Look On The Bright Side Of Life' was played. It seemed that even in death, Patricia could still surprise us. Apparently, she had secretly requested this song from the priest and he'd been sworn to secrecy. When I turned to look at Christy, happy tears were streaming down his cheeks.

Friends and neighbours came in their droves and spoke fondly of Patricia. It was therapeutic to hear how much she meant to them. I met her beloved colleagues from the library, Ronnie and Emma, and I passed on the message she'd left for Ronnie. When I got him on his own, I told him that one of Pat's dying requests was that he should look after Emma. He was taken aback and stuck for words. I smiled at him. 'I'm only the messenger,' I said, knowing that he'd figure it out.

After the burial, we went back to Patricia's house. Christy had arranged caterers so we relaxed, dined and had a few drinks in her honour.

I loved every second of it even though it was the day we buried Patricia. I knew in my heart she'd want us all to enjoy the funeral. This was one of her posthumous wishes coming true already.

*   *   *

In the days afterwards, I was looking through the book of attendees at the funeral mass. I was astonished to see Callum's parents' names. 'Dennis and Jean Whyte' was written clearly and I knew straight away it was them. They didn't come to me to sympathise, but the fact that they were present meant so much to me.

I rang my principal, Maureen. I had seen her at the funeral, but didn't get much of a chance to speak with her. After her sympathies and a few pleasantries, I asked if she'd seen Callum's parents much since his passing.

'No, not much, Debra. They tend to keep to themselves. They've been very quiet, probably still grieving.'

'Yes, no doubt they are. I saw their names in Patricia's funeral book. They were there, but I didn't see them.'

'They might have known her from the library? A lot of the students from school were there.'

'Oh? I must have missed a lot. The church was so packed.'

'I know. There were loads of people standing outside too. She was well known in the community, wasn't she?'

We talked for a while, but what I really wanted from her was information about Callum's family and whether she thought it would be a good idea if I reached out to them.

'When you feel ready, Debra. I'd say they would appreciate that.' I trusted Maureen and I made it my mission to cultivate enough strength to call them. I wanted to work out in my head what I could say to them. It seemed as though I had deserted everyone after Callum's death and I never sympathised with the family, which was really bad form.

Now that I was home I knew I needed to remedy that, or it would haunt me for the rest of my life. I also knew the sooner the better or I might lose my nerve. I couldn't plan to avoid them forever. Despite a population of one and a quarter million, Dublin was geographically small, and I knew one day there was a chance I'd bump into them.

I consulted Cooper's notes regarding the psychology of adolescents. I wondered if there were any answers in them to help me understand why Callum did what he did. All I gleaned from my research was that a teen who lacks resilence and wants to escape from a difficult situation may choose suicide as a solution. Usually, these teenagers had underlying depression and could potentially be unaware of this.

Could Callum have suffered from

depression? He always seemed upbeat and in good form to me, but when I thought really long and hard about it, I remembered he was absent quite frequently. He didn't fall behind because he was both clever and a good listener too. But didn't he miss the fifth-year school trip and the transition-year concert in which he was supposed to perform?

I decided to log into my school account and check the attendance log. I went through his records and those of his siblings in order to compare. It took me almost two hours, but I felt it was worthwhile. I wanted to have a clear picture before I spoke to his parents. I noted that Callum had missed a considerable amount of time since he began secondary school, and had far more absences than any of his siblings. His absences were generally in blocks of anything from three days to a week and often close to the beginning of a new term.

I wondered if there was an illness he suffered from. The absence reasons were mainly cold/flu symptoms or chesty cough. Maybe he was just prone to these types of viruses, but he didn't have asthma or any respiratory condition listed on his profile.

It was only now I could think about him with a clear mindset. Previously, it had been too painful, as the guilt was overwhelming and I couldn't stop judging myself. I focussed on him and his family a lot for a couple of days. Maybe it was my way of distracting myself from thinking about Patricia. I kept forgetting she was gone and half expected her name to appear on my phone whenever I received a call or text.

There was nothing I could do to bring her back and I carried out all of her posthumous requests that were possible. I also checked in with Christy, Daniel and Amy daily to see if they needed anything, but they were coping as best they could. In hindsight, we all had time to prepare for Pat's loss. I just thought I'd have a bit more time, but Patricia was efficient even in death.

At least by focussing my efforts on Callum's family, I could potentially make amends. I wasn't looking for forgiveness from them, as I hadn't forgiven myself yet, but I wanted to make peace with them and console them as best I could. The fact that they'd attended Patricia's funeral gave me hope that they would be willing to speak to me. I talked it over with John and even Phil too when he rang to sympathise. Both of them encouraged me to make the first move with Callum's parents. 'You'll regret it if you don't' were John's words and Phil said, 'Just do it, Debs.'

So I did. The next morning I picked up the phone and rang. I asked to speak to Jean, his mother.

'This is Jean speaking,' she answered.

'Oh, hi Jean. This is Debra Devlin from Sacred Heart. I'm the career-guidance counsellor.'

I just let that information settle and allowed

her to get her bearings.

'Oh, Ms Devlin, yes of course. I'm so sorry to hear about your sister, Patricia. The kids knew her from the library. Would you believe I used to bring them to the toddler story mornings fifteen years ago when she started them?'

'Oh thank you, Jean. Yes, it seems everyone in the locality has a memory of Patricia. I'm so proud of her legacy.' I paused to compose myself. I took a deep breath before continuing. 'I called you today because I wanted to talk about Callum. First of all, I'm so sorry for your loss and I apologise I'm so late with my condolences.' I noticed my hand was shaking. The cause of it may have been down to the vibrations spreading from my rapidly-beating heart.

'Thank you, Ms Devlin. I heard you got a job teaching in Australia or is that just a rumour spread by the sixth-years?'

'Well, to be honest, there's some truth in it. I was in Australia, but I was studying for a postgraduate diploma, not teaching over there.'

'Oh, I see.' Her tone was open and friendly. I felt I could be honest with her. She didn't sound like she was holding me responsible for her son's death or anything, like I'd built myself up to believe.

'Callum's death was the catalyst for my departure, Jean. I don't know how much you know or what you've been told, but he came to see me on the morning of his last day. Did you know that?'

'Oh, well, yes.' She sounded a bit flustered. Why wouldn't she? After a short pause, she continued. 'I knew he went to school for a few hours. He rang me when he came home and I'll never forgive myself for being short with him on the phone. I cut him off because I was busy at work, not to mention annoyed that he'd left school early. He'd missed so many days in fifth year and he'd promised to make more of an effort in sixth year.'

'Yes, I'm aware of his poor attendance. But what I wanted to tell you was that he opened up to me about his problem…his, em, girlfriend who lied about her age.'

'He did? Weren't you his career-guidance counsellor? Why did he…?'

'A lot of the students rely on me as an agony aunt of sorts and share their problems with me. Maybe because I have an office as opposed to a classroom and they feel it's a private space, and I don't know, they seem to trust me. I know Callum did.'

'Yes, I knew he was fond of you. You were one of his favourite teachers. So what did he say on that day and how did he seem?'

'Upset and embarrassed. He didn't like that his peers were calling him names and laughing at his expense. He'd assumed Glenda was older.'

'Yes, we know that now. I think he wanted to talk to me about that when he rang, but like I said, I was short with him and under pressure at work.

He shared his embarrassment with his younger sister, and she told him to rise above it and it would pass. I thought that was good advice, but he didn't listen.'

'I'm so sorry I wasn't more helpful, Jean. On that same day I got word that Patricia had cancer and I was so overcome with sadness that I didn't think to follow up with Callum. I should have informed you or told other staff members. Maybe someone could have gotten through to him?'

'I don't know, Ms Devlin. You may have been the last person he saw at school, but you weren't the last person he spoke to. He rang me that afternoon and then his father, Dennis, who was also at work, but he sensed Callum's mood and took the time to talk things through with him. They even made a plan together to speak to Glenda and her parents to try to put an end to the name-calling, as many of Glenda's friends were responsible for this. He also booked a GP appointment for the following morning, knowing that Callum needed to speak to a professional.'

'Oh, I was under the impression I was the last person he spoke to before he...before he em...'

'No. We were all aware of the situation, but we also knew that Callum had a tendency to overreact and take things personally. He was always the most sensitive person in the family...an emotional child.'

'I'm surprised to hear this. He seemed so "together" in school.'

'I know. He liked school, but he suffered from anxiety during his time in secondary school. Crippling anxiety that had him bed-bound for days. He didn't want anyone knowing and we're a private family, so we never shared his problem with the school. We know now we should have been honest from the start, but we thought we could handle it.'

'I had no idea. He hid it well.'

'He did. Even his close friends weren't aware. We had brought him to the GP over the years on and off, but recently, and in light of it being his leaving-cert year, the GP had prescribed some anti-anxiety medication. Dennis and I didn't want him relying on meds at such a young age, so we went against doctor's orders. As you can imagine, we will regret our decision for the rest of our lives. These past few months have been very hard on us as a family.'

I rushed in with reassurances. 'You thought you were doing the right thing. I understand, Jean. And he was very young for meds like that. They may not have agreed with him either. I'm just so sad to hear that Callum had been suffering in silence during his years in Sacred Heart. Honestly, I never witnessed him having a bad day.'

'I know. So many people have said the same. It's common for children, teens in particular, to behave in one way at school amongst their peers and then let their guards down at home with family. We bore the brunt of his low moods and anxiety, but we loved him so much and miss him every day.' She choked up.

'Jean, I can assure you, he was a happy boy, despite having the problems you mentioned. Thank you for being so open with me. It gives me an understanding of his behaviour, even though I wish I could have intervened more and helped in some way.'

'We all do, Ms Devlin. We all feel like that.'

After the phone call, I cried for the Callum I knew at school and the Callum I didn't know. I cried for his family and friends. She was right, everyone who knew him probably felt they should have done more. It was an inevitable consequence of suicide—guilt and regret for those left behind.

I cried for Patricia too and the gracious way she accepted her fate. She didn't want to go, but made the very best of her last weeks and months. I would be eternally grateful to Christy for breaking his promise to her and letting me spend time with her near the end.

When John arrived home from work, he found me puffy-eyed on my patchwork chair in the living room. Without asking, he made me a hot brandy. Then he cooked dinner and, later that night, climbed into bed beside me to hold me.

I stopped crying and felt safe in his embrace. He didn't sleep in the spare room after that. We slipped back to the way we were. And it was comforting.

Chapter Twenty One

I noticed John was making more of an effort than he ever used to in our relationship. He'd replaced his boring, old, brown coat with a trendy, padded zip-up which made him look at least five years younger. Furthermore, he was organising stuff for us to do at the weekends like picnics in the park, trips to exhibitions and having lunch with friends. He was also very attentive, making sure I had tea and snacks when I was studying and offering to drive me to the university library during rush hour. He knew I hated driving in busy traffic.

My friend, Mae, noticed. 'John seems like a new man since you came home from Australia. I was worried about him for a while. I think he was on the verge of depression, but when he came back from Poland he turned over a new leaf.'

'Maybe it was the joy of reconnecting with his brother, and he was kept busy by helping out in the construction process too,' I mused.

'You know, I think it was when he went to physio and got a plan of action for his physical pain that I noticed the change in him. It was my Seán who recommended physio for him, after assessing his shoulder pains. I think starting the exercises and the swimming gave him a structure, and he could feel the results very quickly.'

'That's amazing,' I said, tucking that little nugget of info about having a plan that delivered results into the back of my mind. I could apply this to psychology when organising follow-up activities for my clients. A million ideas were floating around in my head.

'Yes, he definitely picked up then, but I've never seen him so happy since you returned. I think he's falling for you all over again, Debra!' She winked and I attempted to smile back, but couldn't get past the fact that when he fell for me the first time, it wasn't that dramatic. There were no fireworks. We just happily accepted each other and followed the steps when the time was right.

Even the decision to move in together had been rather unromantic. He'd been living with his mother on the other side of town. When we began spending more time together, he looked into renting a flat on MacMillan Road to be closer to me. Then he stayed with me for a night here and there and we thought it would make better financial sense if he moved in, instead of wasting money on rent.

He'd arrived with relatively few belongings and didn't take over the house in any way. I had everything we needed. I cleared out a wardrobe and some cupboard space for his clothes, tools and manly accessories, which were few and far between—an electric razor, golf clubs and a vast array of hardback sport's stars' biographies.

I had to admit it felt good to have him take

care of me and pay me plenty of attention in recent weeks, because I needed it after everything I'd been through. It was so calm here at home in my own house. I had time to contemplate the last few months, and the more I thought about it, the more I recognised that I did indeed suffer a midlife crisis.

An overdue one—it had been bubbling for a while. I'd been frustrated that nothing was changing. Maybe not having done anything special to mark my fiftieth birthday had something to do with it. John didn't organise anything and it was all kept very low key.

It was only dawning on me now how that had irked me. We should have gone all out and celebrated instead of having a card's night in our house. That said, I hadn't organised anything special for his fiftieth either. We were in the South of France at the time, so I had thought that was special enough. Again, it went to show that neither of us made a huge effort in our relationship to surprise or delight each other.

Then I thought of Phil. Every time I saw him he surprised and delighted me. It was just his nature. He was a naturally exciting person who loved life and his enthusiasm radiated from him. We always laughed so much when we were together, and I missed that.

Before I left Ireland, I remembered how I'd felt that the house was closing in on me and my relationship with John didn't excite me. It was as though we were drifting into old age sooner than we were supposed to. We were only in our fifties, our midlife years. Old age was far off in the distance, or at least it should have been.

I was completely consumed by school work and admin. In fact, everything in my life had seemed static before I left, but it didn't hit me until the night I found myself wandering around the street at four in the morning.

That was why my trip abroad was so worthwhile. It had opened up my eyes to what the world had to offer and I certainly wanted to see more of it. I wanted to return to Thailand some day and I'd love to see more of Australia, apart from beautiful Sydney. But what I wanted more than anything was to focus on my career. That precious time in Citywest Uni had fuelled my hunger for further studies.

I knew I had a gift for helping people and I could make a difference. I thought about how family members relied on me for advice, how the students at school looked to me when they had problems and how the staff sought me out when the stress of teaching became too much. I seemed to be able to offer support to those around me, except Callum, of course.

Although clearly I had failed him, I shouldn't let that failure nullify my successes. Maybe he was the one who got away. It sounded like he'd resisted numerous offers of help and not just mine. I would never get over that defeat, but I would no longer allow it to hold me back. It could well prove to be impossible, but I vowed that I would work on one day trying to forgive myself.

The idea of setting up my own practice appealed to me. And I wanted to do it here on MacMillan Road, my home, where I was rooted. I was well-known in the community due being a teacher in the local school and I wasn't sure, but maybe by opening up a practice here, I could help kids like Callum and their parents. Perhaps this was how I was going to atone for past failures.

*   *   *

John had booked dinner for us in a local restaurant on Saturday night with our friends, George and Mae. He had started buying new clothes in recent weeks and he looked very handsome in a navy suit with a white shirt. Even Mae complimented his appearance while giving me a sneaky wink and a nod.

They always enjoyed it when we got together as a foursome. They'd known Patricia and her family, so we shared some funny stories about Pat's antics in the past. They were very proud of their son, Seán the doctor, and Mae boasted about him to no end. This time myself and John shared a sneaky wink and a nod when Mae rambled on and on.

I noticed John was trying it on more too. I wasn't always in the mood and he understood that. He wasn't pushy, but he let me know that he still wanted me. He put my occasional refusal down to grief, but I knew the real reason. He wasn't Phil, and although I loved John and appreciated him, I couldn't get Phil out of my head, especially when myself and John were getting intimate.

Phil was a looming presence in my mind, but I didn't know what to do about it. He was allowing me space to grieve since Patricia's passing and he told me to call him as soon as I was ready. But I knew if I called him I'd tell him every detail about Pat's death and it would be triggering for him. He'd worked very hard to accept what happened to Nicole, so I wanted to spare him the ordeal of rehashing old memories if I were to share my grief with him.

We still texted, but I didn't pick up the phone to ring him. I wanted to, but I knew the longer I left it, the easier it would be for him to hear that I'd reunited with John. He'd probably assume it by now anyway, if he wasn't completely preoccupied with his travel plans. I knew he was working overtime to fund his travels too, so it was likely he didn't have much time to think about me.

Knowing him, he'd meet someone in Bali. The thoughts of it pierced my heart, but I believed I was in the right place at the right time and John was probably the right person for me right now.

It was just as well I felt like that because two weeks later on his birthday, he arrived home with a bunch of red roses and a ring!

'John! What the heck are you doing?' I

screamed with laughter when he got down on one knee. I was sitting on my patchwork chair in the living room reading a book on cognitive psychology, when he burst through the door with the flowers in one hand and a ring box in the other.

'Debra, I love you. I'm so glad you came back to me and I don't want to lose you again. You make me so happy.' I was in stitches at this stage, but he continued regardless. 'Will you marry me?' And he opened the beautiful box from Weir and Sons' Jewellers. A tiny diamond twinkled by the light of the evening sun shining through the window.

'John! I can't believe you! But we never even discussed this!' He'd never surprised me like this before. Usually, I'd know what he was thinking even before he articulated it himself, but I hadn't seen this coming!

Then he surprised me even more when he said, 'Go on, Debra, say yes!' An image of Phil flashed before my eyes. That was just like something he'd say.

I was stunned though, and beyond overwhelmed that John had even been thinking along these lines. I hadn't. Despite my racing mind of late, I'd simply been trying to get through one day and onto the next. But this...this was unexpected to say the least.

Was this something I'd secretly wanted? I knew I'd always wished John was more spontaneous and he'd proven of late that he could be. He joined in with my surprised laughter and I couldn't bring myself to spoil the fun by saying no. I just couldn't resist feeling the unexpected joy of this wonderful moment.

'Yes, I'll marry you!' He took my hand, pulled me up off the chair and we kissed with intent…like lovers. Like we hadn't ever kissed before. It sort of felt like the first time. For me, anyway.

Chapter Twenty Two

I got a message from Phil. I read and reread the message while holding the phone close to my heart.

Phil
Hey Debs, hope all well. Forgive the lengthy text, but I'll be off the radar for a while. Booked a 6 wk meditation thingy. If I refuse the vow of silence, we can talk after that! You're still on my mind, Phil

I was grateful he would be uncontactable for a while. It meant I wouldn't have to share my wedding news with him just yet. I imagined it would be easier to tell all when a few things were organised. At the moment it was just a proposal and a ring.

Oh, who was I kidding? I didn't want to tell Phil for fear of hurting him. It would come as a shock to him. At the same time, I presumed he'd be happy for me and would want the best for me. Neither of us would have wanted to continue a long-distance relationship. He would meet someone too. I was sure of it. Probably in Bali...some lone, middle-aged traveller who'd look better than me in a bikini.

I had confidence in his looks and personality that he wouldn't get lonely on his travels. It was flattering that he was still contacting me and interested in remaining in touch. He was still on my mind too and maybe that was why I didn't feel ready to share the news of John's proposal with him.

*   *   *

Everyone was delighted to hear about our engagement. Mae organised a party for us and we received flowers from John's office. The teachers did a collection for me even though I didn't feel like a member of staff any more. Technically, I had been due back in September, but ended up getting approval for unpaid leave from the board of management. It covered me until Christmas so I'd be expected back to school in January.

This would be enough time for me to complete exams and organise a schedule to observe professional therapists in practice. I wanted to choose wisely and make the right connections. I would initially shadow an experienced practitioner until I was fully qualified.

I also needed time to research venues for what would one day be my own therapeutic practice. I'd spotted a small premises in the city centre that was for rent. I had hoped for something more local, but couldn't find anything suitable. This one had a reception and space for two therapy rooms, which I loved, as it would keep costs down to split the rent with another therapist. Most counselling practices offered a choice of therapists, so having two consultation rooms made sense. Maybe I was getting ahead of myself, though. I needed to pass my exams first.

I bought a new navy and green, stripy dress for the engagement party. John wore his navy suit, this time with a colourful tie, a gift from Patricia that he never got to wear in her presence. My dress was long and flowy, yet still casual. I never tended to go for glamour—comfort was king in my books. Nevertheless, I received lots of compliments on the night.

Amy brought the kids, Daniel brought his new girlfriend. I noticed, with secret delight, that it was the first time I'd seen Christy smile since Patricia passed away.

A few of our neighbours, together with John's work-friends were there. We drank and toasted Patricia as well as the happy couple. John was over the moon and made a speech, which included berating himself for not doing this ten years ago. Everyone laughed, while I wondered if I would have accepted his proposal ten years ago. I wasn't entirely sure, but now seemed like the right time. Everything was falling into place.

He would support me with my career plans, it made our family and friends happy and I felt that Patricia would understand why it made sense too. The only person I tried not to think about was Phil. And that wasn't too difficult with him being out of reach, offline and thousands of miles away locked up with Buddhist monks...

*   *   *

Over the next while, I achieved first class honours in my end-of-semester exams. I also obtained my licence to practise, which meant I could start work experience. Now I just had to find the right location to do this.

The wedding plans took a back seat. I noticed John slipping into old habits after the excitement of the engagement party. He'd gone on a golf outing with work and his shoulder became painful again. Instead of revisiting the physio, he decided to do more exercises as they'd cured him previously. However, this time the movement seemed to make it worse. His physiotherapist was away on holidays for two weeks, so he suffered while he waited for his return.

He couldn't go swimming either and his pool membership lapsed. He said he'd renew it once he got his pain remedied, but neither of us knew how long that would take. I'd noticed a change in him when I returned home initially, when he was constantly surprising me and impressing me. But lately, he was inclined to sit in and complain about his aches and pains.

I encouraged him to see a different physio because it was proving difficult to get an appointment, but he insisted he wanted to see the same guy. Forever loyal was John, even if it meant enduring pain for longer than he needed to.

I was riding high with my exam results. I'd

been in touch with Cooper who was still offering me help from uni in Sydney should I need it. I also realised Phil would have finished his meditation course by now. I just wanted to let him know about my exam result as he'd been so supportive of my studies, and even proud of me. I texted.

Debra
Hi Phil, I hope you're feeling zen after your meditation retreat. Just letting you know, I received first class honours in my exams! Debra ;-)

Later that evening, he replied.

Phil
Wow! Wow! Wow! Congrats! You're an inspiration!

Debra
Thanks, Phil. I'm thrilled! I'm looking into setting up my own practice now

Phil
In Sydney??!

Debra
In Dublin :-)

Phil
Haha..thought so

And then a few minutes later, my phone beeped again.

Phil
Worth a try, though!

I didn't expect him to show an interest like this in me. I thought he would have moved on with somebody else by now, but it sounded like he was still eager to see me again and maybe rekindle something. I didn't reply. I didn't want to get into a lengthy back-and-forth, because I hadn't yet told him about myself and John. I just didn't feel like broaching the subject at this time.

Patricia's daughter, Amy, seemed to be beyond excited about our pending nuptials. Maybe it was a distraction from her grief. She called over regularly to check if we needed help with any of the organising. I asked John what we could delegate to her, but neither of us were quite sure what needed to be done.

He had bought the engagement ring and in his mind, he was done. The rest, it seemed, was up to me. All I knew was that I wanted a small, simple wedding and I wasn't in a mad hurry either. I was upfront with Amy and she told me not to worry. She was "on it". First of all she was going to look into venues and once that was chosen, she assured me the rest would fall into place. And I believed her.

*   *   *

I was more interested in finding a venue for my counselling and therapeutic practice. I kept gravitating towards the little basement in the city centre. I liked the location first and foremost. It was less than two miles from the centre of town, but still close enough to be considered the city centre. There was street parking outside and plenty of bus and LUAS stops too.

I wanted local clients and although it wasn't on MacMillan Road, it was only a short drive or bus ride away, so I could still advertise locally. I arranged a viewing and went on my own. I was sure John would have come along had I asked, but this was my baby, my project and my business, so I went alone.

It had been a dental surgery previously, but all the machinery and extra sinks et cetera had been removed, so it was a clean slate. The walls were bright and white. There were two small consultation rooms, a reception and a tiny bathroom. It was perfect, in my opinion, and I could picture myself there.

Although it was a basement, there were small rectangular windows in both of the consultation rooms and the glass-panelled door allowed natural light into the reception. The only massive, big, huge, urgent problem was the cost.

Now that the travelling bug was out of my system (for a little while anyway) and the mortgage was almost paid on my house, I could use my teaching salary to pay for rent. But, of course, this would mean having to return to teaching in January as planned. I secretly worried

I wouldn't have the time to dedicate to the amount of work experience that my course required. As soon as I arrived home from the viewing, I rang Maureen.

We discussed my plans at length and she was eager to help. She understood that I had course requirements to fulfil and told me she'd try to accommodate me.

My future dreams didn't include a return to Sacred Heart, but I needed money for those dreams to become a reality. I could have asked John to chip in, but I wanted to be independent and do this on my own.

True to her word, Maureen rang the following morning with a bright idea. She had consulted with my temporary replacement teacher and ascertained that she would be prepared to job-share with me for the remainder of the school year. This would mean working part-time hours and sharing the workload. I was intrigued by the offer and impressed with Maureen's resourcefulness, but didn't accept it straight away.

I put my business hat on and made a pros and cons list. I did the maths to check if a reduction to half pay would be enough to cover the rent. I took into account the income from the lease of the second consultation room if I managed to secure the basement clinic as this could make up the shortfall in salary. When I double-checked the numbers, I realised a job-share could prove to be a viable solution.

The first thing I did was tell John. I was so enthusiastic, he kept asking me to slow down. By the time I finished, my excitement was palpable and if he had found a flaw in my plan, I think I may have dumped him on the spot. He said he'd need to see the venue before agreeing.

Furthermore, he was very happy at the prospect of me going back to school. He said I was usually at my happiest when immersed in teaching. I smiled, even though an image of Phil kissing me on his couch flashed before my eyes. Wasn't that when I was at my happiest? I blinked it away.

Not that I needed it, but it felt good to have his approval. This was an independent venture that I wanted to see through on my own. The feminist in me was emerging, or maybe the travelling had given me the confidence to know that I could succeed without a partner.

After some more running through the figures with an accountant and an assurance from Mae's son, Doctor Seán, that there was a plethora of therapists seeking venues in Dublin to lease, I put down a deposit. As of next month, I could start moving furniture in and begin decorating the place to suit my needs. I just needed a suitable name for my new clinic.

When I described it to Christy, he was taken with the idea of a basement therapy clinic. He jokingly suggested "Debra's Dungeon" or "Into the Darkness", even though I clarified it was actually bright and airy. Nevertheless, I liked the alliteration in his first suggestion. John was there too and offered "Debra's Den". We all laughed, and somehow, a potential name for my new business was created in the midst of the fun.

I was attracted to Triple D Therapy Rooms. Of course it would be subject to approval from my future partner and I really hoped he or she would have the initial D in their name. "DDD" or "Triple D" which stood for Debra's Discussion Den, was rolling off our tongues, but also reminding me, and probably John too, of my bra size. I wondered if I could get away with it. On the plus side, it was memorable, and that was a good start.

Chapter Twenty Three

B eing back in school, albeit part-time, was intense. After the first day of greetings and sharing stories of my studies in Australia, I pretty much continued where I'd left off. I could see my replacement teacher had been struggling to keep up to date with her records, so I was hoping the change to part-time would straighten this out and after a few weeks, it did.

It was a little tricky to explain to staff members why I'd left so suddenly after Callum's death. They knew I'd been the last person he saw at school and I had documented our encounter a couple of days later, when of course, it was too late. I got the impression that some teachers were disappointed in my actions, so I decided to elaborate in the staff room one day during my first week back.

'I'm sorry for leaving you all on the lurch following the death of Callum. Needless to say, it hit me hard and, to tell the truth, I had a mini breakdown. I very hastily booked a flight abroad to escape from the sadness. I just found out that my sister had cancer on the same day that Callum died. I suppose it was all too much for me to take in.'

'But you didn't come back, Debra. That's what I don't understand,' pleaded Alison, one of the younger members of staff who'd often come to me looking for advice. She probably needed me at that time and had felt deserted.

'I know. I was traumatised, Alison and I got a sick note until the end of term. That was when I got the idea of finishing my studies abroad. What's more, my relationship was in trouble too, so I stayed away and immersed myself in a postgrad in Sydney.'

'And what made you decide to come back?' asked a new member of staff who didn't know me from Adam, but was enjoying my story nonetheless.

'Well, as I said, my sister was ill and I wanted to spend some time with her towards the end. And I got my relationship with John back on track too,' I said as I held up my right hand to show my engagement ring. After the obligatory congratulations, I continued.

'Now that I'm qualified, my goal is to set up my own therapy practice. But rent in Dublin is expensive so I came back to help fund that dream. Also, I wasn't proud of the way I'd left, so it feels like I have unfinished business to attend to.'

'Oh no, Debra, we totally understand and we're delighted to have you back,' piped up Maureen, who was gulping down her coffee because she had a visitor at reception. Before she raced out, I wanted to clarify something. 'I meant unfinished business with the students, Maureen. I left them in their grief without any explanation and I still feel awful about that.'

'There wasn't much you could do, Debra. They had to go through it to feel their emotions and ride it out. There wasn't much any of us could do. Many of Callum's close friends and siblings remained out of school for a couple of weeks afterwards. They returned to complete exams at the end of term. The summer holidays came so quickly then, but they had each other to lean on, and I think that's how they coped,' said Maureen.

'Agreed,' said Alison. 'They didn't want interference from us teachers. They had their own ways of getting through it. You didn't let them down.'

'Thanks guys,' I said, although nothing they offered alleviated my guilt. I did try to broach the subject with my current sixth-years, given many of them would have known Callum. However, once I began mentioning his name, I detected an air of discomfort from the students. I took that as a hint that they'd rather I discontinued. So instead, I shared with them my office hours in case any of them wanted to talk.

It was a while before they started coming to me for advice and trusting me again. Maybe that was due to my part-time hours and not seeing me so often. But when they eventually did approach me, I felt like things were returning to normal. Relationships were getting rebuilt, along with the formation of new ones.

I only worked Monday, Tuesday and every

second Wednesday, so I had time to commit to Triple D Therapy Rooms. Christy had lots of useful contacts for me from being in the building trade. He got me a plumber and a painter and took care of any other odd jobs himself.

The reception was gleaming with white walls, a black soft leather couch in the waiting area, a coffee table filled with mental-health magazines and a desk for my non-existent receptionist. My consultation room had been designed by me. Again, white walls for a fresh appearance and two colourful, fabric chairs. One had navy and green stripes like the pattern on the dress I'd worn to my engagement party, and the other was blue and grey. They looked inviting, and I popped a tiny cushion on each for extra comfort.

I had storage for all of my files and ordered some for the other consultation room, which would soon be filled by a therapist recommended by Dr Seán. A familiar name caught my eye on the client-list. It was Ronnie from the library, a colleague of Patricia's, and I hoped everything was okay.

I was delighted that my new colleague, Dr Dominick Delany, approved the name, Triple D Therapy Rooms. We figured people could decide for themselves what the Ds stood for and which of our names it represented. It could also potentially be something related to doctoring, discussion or discourse. I personally liked "Debra's Discussion Den" and that's what I would be telling people it stood for. I giggled every time I thought of my bra-size, though.

*   *   *

I knew I should have been putting more of my time and effort into wedding-planning, but teaching and setting up the practice zapped my energy. John wasn't doing a tap for it so I didn't feel too guilty. It was like he'd forgotten he'd asked me to marry him. He never got back into the rhythm of his physio exercises, but did return to swimming once a week. He also went golfing every other weekend, so it seemed like he was enjoying a social life without me.

Everyone kept asking if we were planning a spring wedding. I hadn't a clue so I referred to Amy and asked if this was a possibility. She laughed initially before telling me that any decent wedding venue for a party of fifty or more would be booked up six months in advance. She'd been looking into summer dates for us.

I thought fifty sounded a lot for a small wedding, but when I counted our relations, close friends and the colleagues we'd want to invite, I realised it would turn out to be a little over fifty. I'd been to so many weddings over the years, but didn't want to get guilted into inviting people just because I'd been to theirs. Myself and John were in our fifties, so we wouldn't fret about stuff like that. We'd just aim to please ourselves.

*   *   *

As I was shadowing experienced therapists wherever I could clock up hours, my phone never stopped ringing. On my non-teaching days, I would travel around to different clinics, observing therapy sessions. Sometimes a last minute approval would arrive and I'd have to drop everything and go, so my phone was always within reach.

However, I got a surprise when one of those phone calls ended up being Phil. When his name lit up on my screen, I put my hand to my heart to calm it down before answering.

'Phil! Hi! Long time no hear! I thought maybe you'd decided to return to the monastery to join the monkhood!' I joked.

'Hey Debra, it's good to hear your voice and eh, I don't think the monks would have me!' he replied with a chuckle. 'But no, the meditation course wasn't like that at all. It was deep and I got so much out of it. I'll tell you about it another time, though. I rang because I wanted to ask you something. Can you talk?'

My heart rate accelerated and butterflies thundered through my tummy. What was happening? What did Phil want?

'Yes,' I said. 'I can talk. Go ahead.'

'I had an idea,' he said. 'My six months of travel is nearing an end. I've to go back to work soon, but eh, I was planning to take in a bit of

Europe before I return. My flight takes me through London. Now I know it's been a while, and you've settled into your old life back there in Dublin, so this is a longshot, but...'

He paused as if wondering whether to continue or not. Was he losing his nerve?

'Go on, Phil. I'd like to hear your idea,' I encouraged him.

'Well, would you like to meet me in London for a weekend in February? I should get there Wednesday, the 14th. I'm sure you've got plans or maybe you're back with John? I, eh, don't want to be presumptuous, like it's been quite a while since we've spoken, but if you were free and you'd like to meet, I'll be there for a few days. And eh, well, yeah, that's it really...'

Oh? Hmmm... My heart continued to pound. This man could do things to me. That was for sure. A weekend in London? Easy—I'd be there in an hour, wouldn't need to pack much, a little city break... My mind was racing. I glanced at the calendar on my desk and confirmed that would be my short week at work, so I wouldn't need to request time off. Tempting, so very tempting...

I realised the silence was becoming awkward and I didn't want to say no. I really didn't want to pass up the opportunity to see Phil without a thirty-hour flight to Sydney. London would only take a measly hour to get to. Ohhh, I really didn't want to say no.

'Yes!' I exclaimed, after an unbearably, long,

uncomfortable pause.

'What?' he shouted into the phone. I had to distance it from my ear. 'Did you say yes, Debs?' he bellowed again.

'I did, Phil. I'd love to see you!' I meant it. 'I'll look into flights today and let you know.'

'Well, I'll be arriving in Heathrow around two o'clock in the afternoon if that helps?'

'Perfect, Phil, I'm sure I can arrange an afternoon flight. I'll be in touch, okay?'

'That's magic, Debra! I didn't think you'd say yes, but I'm chuffed you did. Really excited about seeing you!' His enthusiasm and gratitude was palpable.

'Me too, Phil, me too!'

*   *   *

I was sitting on my patchwork chair in the living room when he hung up. I rocked back and forth, even though it wasn't a rocking chair. The ear-to-ear beam loosened its grip on my cheeks, and in a matter of seconds, my expression turned to one of horror. Oh no, what have I done? That was a massively spontaneous thing to do. I just agreed to meet Phil in London for a long weekend...on Valentine's Day! *Hmmm...*

I rocked more on my static chair and wondered how I would break this news to John— my fiance!

And then I realised I couldn't. I couldn't tell John that I was meeting the man of my dreams for a romantic getaway in London. I couldn't do that, so there was only one thing to do.

I had to tell John that I couldn't marry him. That would solve my problem about having to tell my fiance about Phil. If I followed through with this, I wouldn't have a fiance to tell.

And then I could go with a somewhat clear conscience and enjoy a romantic Valentine's Day... with Phil.

Swoon...

I mean...what's happening?!

Chapter Twenty Four

It was the allure of his shapely calves that I couldn't resist. And his easy-going, outgoing, larger-than-life personality. Not to mention his curls, his smile, his face and his hands. But mainly the way he could make me feel. And the way he could make me laugh. Oh…and the way he made everything seem exciting, even if it was just a drink in the local pub, or a walk in the park or a quick chat on the phone. He could ignite sparks from the simplest things. That was the wonder of Phil…or maybe just his effect on me.

I'd allowed myself to "fall in" again with John. I was doing what was easy, whatever required the least amount of effort and kept everyone happy, so I could focus on other things. John was a close friend and practically a family member at this stage. He had my back and was always there for me when I needed him.

But there was no escaping the fact that he wasn't the man of my dreams. So why was I marrying him? Was I afraid of being alone? No. Was he? Yes. Did I want a companion in my maturing years? No. I wanted lots of friends and companions, and colleagues and clients. My life was so full.

Did John really love me, or was he so invested in our long-running relationship and our mutual families that it was too much like hard work to end it and start afresh? I was going to find out. I planned to break the news to him the same evening I committed to meeting Phil in London. I would do it after he came home from swimming. I checked our brandy levels and was confident I'd have enough for refills, if required.

*   *   *

When he arrived home we had a light dinner. He complained that his shoulder was "at him", so he informed me he was going to give up swimming for a while. I reminded him about the expense of the monthly membership fee for the pool, but he dismissed my concerns.

After dinner I told him I was going to have a brandy and offered him one. He thought it might help his shoulder pain, so he accepted. I told him the swimming or the prescribed exercises from the physio might better help his shoulder, but he dismissed me for the second time that evening.

We sat on the couch and I turned to him.

'John, you're not going to like what I'm about to say.'

'What? Is it golf? Are you going to suggest my shoulder pain is down to the golf? Is that it?'

'No. Although now that you mention it, it's probably putting a strain on it. Speak to the physio about it at your next appointment.'

He sighed as if I was nagging, even though we both knew I wasn't. His mother had nagged him relentlessly so he was hyper-sensitive about it. She was dead and gone, but it actually seemed to me like he missed the intrusive nagging from time to time. Maybe it reminded him of his mother and he found it comforting…

'John, I have something to tell you.'

He picked up the remote to hurry me along. 'Yeah, go on, Deb.'

'I don't think we should get married.'

He dropped the remote.

'What?' he barked, as if that was the last thing he expected me to say.

'I don't think we're enough in love to get married,' I clarified.

'What?' he asked again.

'I think we're more comfortable companions than lovers and I don't want to marry my comfortable companion. I do, however, want to remain friends with you. Does that make sense?'

'No, not in the slightest. Comfortable what? I'm not a hot water bottle, Debra.'

I put my hand to my mouth. That made me laugh a little, but I stopped myself.

'I know. I know that, John. Look, I think you got wind of the fact that I met someone in Australia. That was why I asked you for a break from our relationship. I didn't want to go into detail at the time, but I had a fling, John, with an Aussie guy.'

He put his hand to his head. 'Ah Deb, stop! Don't be telling me this. I don't want to know.

You're home now and you seem over it. Don't go there now. You don't have to admit anything to me.'

'I know that. But the thing is, he'll be in London in February and I've agreed to meet him. So, you see, John, I can't marry you. Not if I'm meeting him while we're engaged. It wouldn't be right, so I have to break it off. I'm sorry.'

He still didn't believe me. I could tell from both his silence and wide-eyed, bewildered expression.

'Look, John, I know this is hard to take in, but we can work something out. I know we can. I'll move into the spare room for now to give us a chance to process things. I'll ring people and let them know the wedding's off. You shouldn't be lumped with any of that.'

'Deb, is this another midlife crisis? I've heard they're like mice. There's never only one of them.'

'No, John. I don't think it is. I'm just listening to my gut...'—I paused and gulped because I got a little choked up mid-sentence—'...and my heart... and they're both telling me to meet Phil in London, and end it with you. I'm sorry. You've been so good to me and the family since Patricia's passing. I appreciate you and I love you, but I don't want to marry you.'

'Okay,' he replied. Oh? Did he feel the same? I was astonished as I waited for him to elaborate. 'We don't have to get married. I mean, it was a silly idea. At our age and everything. Sure, what are we trying to prove? We can just carry on as we are, Debra. Would that suit you better? Seriously, I wouldn't be too disappointed if we parked the wedding plans.'

I exhaled and let out a jaded sigh. So the truth came out. Obviously, I hadn't just been imagining his apathy.

'John, I want to be straight with you so you'll be left with no doubts. Marriage or no marriage, I want to end our relationship. This isn't easy for me because you mean so much to me. But it needs to be said. I need to let you know how I really feel and what I actually want. I'm going to London to meet Phil and I'm telling you this because I respect you...and I love you.'

'So, what you're saying is, you're leaving me for a fling. Our years together mean nothing to you! You're packing it all in for a meaningless frolic...' He stopped right there and turned away from me on the couch. He downed his brandy before getting up to fetch another. He didn't offer me one and we said no more.

He needed time to process my revelations and I understood that. He picked up the remote again and turned on the TV. He didn't speak. He was done for the evening, I could tell, so I went into the other room to give him space.

*   *   *

When I broke the news to Christy and Amy, Christy cried. He'd been so emotional since Patricia's death. He was crying at both good and bad news these days. His new puppy, which Patricia had insisted he got for company after her death, rushed to his side to comfort him by licking his fingers. As for Amy, she only wanted the best for me. Much like her mother, whatever I wanted, she encouraged. She squeezed my arm before I left and whispered to me to send a few pics of Phil and me loved up in London.

In the following days, John tried to no end to convince me to change my mind. He couldn't understand my decision when "everything was going so well" as he put it. I told him I agreed that things were working well and we were comfortable, but I wanted more than that. More than comfort. And every time I tried to elaborate, he rolled his eyes and accused me of having a midlife crisis.

Maybe he was right. Maybe I was. I was willing to give up security, stability and companionship for a rendezvous with my heartthrob in London. I was fully aware that myself and Phil were not going to make it as a couple. He was so rooted in Sydney with his job, family, friends and routine. He was happy there and I couldn't imagine him living elsewhere.

After securing Triple D Therapy Rooms and the finances to start my own clinic with my earnings from teaching, there was no way I would uproot now. I had family and good friends here, together with plenty of contacts to keep me going.

Although I loved life in Sydney, I felt it was here in Dublin that I was meant to be.

Strangely, I felt like I belonged ever since I'd returned. It was like a city with claws. It had begrudgingly let me go in my deranged, half-drunken stupor, but now that I was back, I was gripped. Locked tightly in its hold, both captured and captivated.

*   *   *

John eventually accepted that I wasn't going to change my London plans. He moved his things over to his late mother's house. In an effort to help him, Christy suggested that he should renovate the old house now that he had experience of working on his brother's house in Poland. He even offered to help, with being a builder himself and having the right contacts. I secretly hoped John would accept, as it would be a great, all-consuming project for both of them to get stuck into. There was no doubt they both needed a major distraction at this time, so something like this could prove to be therapeutic.

We hugged when John came to collect the last of his stuff. He said he didn't want to let me go and I told him I would always be there for him. He also asked to see me when I returned home from London, so we made a loose arrangement to meet for lunch in late February.

After weeks of quiet excitement, there was only one thing left for me to do—pack my things and get to the airport on time!

*   *   *

The massive bear hug I received in Heathrow from a very tanned and even more handsome Phil than I remembered, validated my decision to leave John. Phil asked for my consent to kiss me, because he didn't know if I was single or not. I didn't answer him. I just grabbed his face between my hands, stared into his eyes and smiled. His eyebrows were lighter from the sun in Bali and his hair an even shinier shade of grey.

He stared back and returned my knowing smile. Then we both leaned in at the same time and our lips met. I immediately felt warm ripples of yearning flow through my bloodstream. The meeting of our lips awakened something in me, something I hadn't truly felt since the last time I saw Phil in Sydney Airport. It didn't take us long to build momentum and the internal ripples swirled with increasing urgency. I sensed a familiar desire in my body that only Phil could elicit, and I went with it. I relished it. I felt it.

We hugged after we kissed and held each other tight. It almost felt like we were holding each other up, steadying our stance, both weakened by the strength of our kiss.

*   *   *

He'd made dinner reservations at the hotel he was staying in. I hadn't booked any accommodation, with the assumption that I'd hop into whatever bed Phil was sleeping in. He was delighted when I shared this and laughed when I apologised for being presumptuous.

He relayed every detail about his trip to Bali and beyond, and sold it to me like an expert travel agent. Now he was doing a brief tour of Europe before returning to Australia. He also said he planned to make international travel a yearly adventure for the rest of his life and hinted that maybe I could join him in the future. I assured him I was planning to make time for travel too, now that I had the confidence to fly to the other side of the world on my own.

London was magical. We spent a lot of time reconnecting in our hotel bed and Phil told me he'd missed my triple D bras and their complicated hooks and clasps.

We also managed to fit in a show in the West End and a visit to Madame Tussauds. We shared our mutual love of food over a Valentine's dinner in the hotel bar and clinked our glasses of champagne with promises to see each other again in the near future.

When our time together came to an end, we both welled up saying goodbye at the airport. He was getting a train to Paris and embarking on a ten-day interrailing tour of Europe. He told me it was a cheap and cheerful way to see lots of cities, and he loved train travel.

He gave me a CD as a parting gift. More

music he'd discovered that didn't bring back memories of Nicole, so it was safe. He said a mad American hippie gave it to him in Bali and it was the best present he'd ever received. He went and bought me the very same CD in London, thinking I'd appreciate it too. He warned me not to expect any current music trends, proudly admitting that this one was "old school". I laughed when I saw that he'd gone to the trouble of getting it gift wrapped...it was a CD!

We kissed at the airport as though it was the last time. Neither of us knew for sure if it was, so we covered all eventualities just in case. It was hard saying goodbye, but we seemed to have a mutual understanding of where we each belonged—me in Dublin in Triple D's and Phil in Sydney beside Mick O'Shea's. We reluctantly, but graciously, allowed each other part in the opposite direction, with the rapture of these precious few days together still palpable. We promised to keep in touch.

For the first time in our relationship I appreciated our maturing years, because we were at a stage of our lives where we knew exactly what we wanted. I felt grateful to have come this far and reached this pivotal age, having so many life lessons and experience under my belt. How many people were lucky enough to realise this? Patricia's image briefly came to mind.

Right there and then at Heathrow Airport, I vowed to lead a full and exhilarating life. I would live for both of us. I would embark on many exciting adventures. I wouldn't allow fear to get the better of me. I'd challenge myself and always be a few steps outside my comfort zone. This would allow me to grow and learn something new every day. I'd have to park my regrets up to now, in case they held me back. I'd tell my clients to do the same.

With each day that passed, I would recognise that I was a survivor and lucky to be alive. I'd find a way to spread this simple message of gratitude. I'd do it for me and others who needed to hear it. But mostly, I'd do it for Patricia.

Chapter Twenty Five

I felt a sense of overwhelming pride on the day I cut the ribbon at the front door of Triple D Therapy Rooms. Amy insisted on an official opening party, assuring me that's what Patricia would have wanted. I didn't object. I couldn't. I was too happy to say no.

It was a joint venture with my new colleague, Dominick, who was sharing the rental cost with me. He was just as excited as me about Triple D because it was his first private clinic. Up to now he'd been a consultant in a public hospital, so he had both experience and a long list of contacts which could only be a good thing.

A small crowd clapped as Amy's kids helped me snip the ribbon. In a way it would be a family affair, because Amy agreed to become our receptionist. We could both feel Patricia's blessings in the air regarding this decision.

I was taken by surprise when John showed up to wish me well. And even more so when it transpired that a tall, attractive woman was accompanying him. I hadn't heard much from him since my weekend in London as we never got round to our planned meeting. I got the odd bit of news about him from Christy and knew that he'd gone ahead with the proposed house renovation. It was fast becoming an obsession for both of them or, as Christy put it, a labour of love.

I was happy for him. It was going to bring in an income too, as he was creating a small apartment to rent within the house. I was proud of him for taking it on and glad he wasn't letting our breakup get the better of him.

'Congrats, Debra,' he said and raised his glass of champagne. 'I know this is what you've always wanted.'

'Thanks, John. It's great to see you. I wasn't sure if you'd come!' I had mentioned it in passing to Christy that it would be nice to see him, but wasn't sure if the message got passed on.

'How have you been?' I asked.

'Busy, but good. This renovation project with Christy will either make me or break me,' he laughed with raised eyebrows as he rubbed his shoulder.

'Oh, you still have that pain, have you?' I sympathised.

'It comes and goes,' he said. 'But hopefully my new tenant will help remedy it!'

'Oh? You have someone lined up to move in? That was quick!'

'Ewa's friend moved here from Poland. She's over there talking to Mae. She's a massage therapist and I reckon I'll be her first client!'

'Oh, that's wonderful, John. I hope you get some relief from that. Did she, em, come alone?' I was just curious...

'She's recently separated. Ewa said she's

looking for a fresh start.'

'Ah, I see', I said, thinking it sounded like a master move on Ewa's part to set her friend up with an eligible bachelor in Dublin. However, I kept my thoughts to myself and wished him well.

*   *   *

I felt empowered to be embarking on my new business venture as a single woman. Little did I know that my spontaneous decision to leave Dublin after Callum's passing would eventually inspire such fire in me. Despite my initial doubts, the benefits of travel outnumbered the drawbacks. Of course that was mainly due to the wonderful people I met along the way like Cooper, Ned, Amara, and of course, Phil.

I'd sent out free therapy vouchers to a select few. In fact, all five sessions went to Callum's family. I just thought they must still be grieving and money was often a reason why people didn't engage with therapy in the first place. I had specialised in grief counselling as an add-on to my course and I really wanted to help the family in some way, since letting Callum down. There were five family members left and I hoped to see each one individually in the clinic for an hour each.

His mother was the first to book her appointment. She was also my first client in Triple D, although I was still under the watchful eye of my supervisor. When she set foot in the door, we both welled up. 'Thank you,' she said. 'No, thank

YOU for coming,' I insisted. 'How are you, Jean?' I gestured for her to take a seat.

She sat opposite me and sighed. 'Well, it doesn't get any easier, Ms Devlin,' she said.

'Please, call me Debra. It's been a year now, hasn't it? His anniversary must have been hard.'

'Yes, it was like attending the funeral all over again. Seeing everyone there at the church brought it all back.'

'I can imagine. Was it cathartic in any way? Did you feel supported when you saw the huge crowd in the church?' I was one of them and could confirm it was mobbed.

'I know I should have, but no, not really. It just brought it all back. The shock of when he died. It was me who found him, you know.'

'Yes, I know that, Jean. It must be difficult to erase the image from your mind. Have you tried anything to help that?'

'Like what? The only thing I've done is get sleeping tablets from the doctor to help me get through the night. That's how I'm coping to be honest.'

'I see. I meant hypnotherapy or PTSD counselling, perhaps? There are very specific things you can do to come to terms with the traumatic memories.'

'Are the sleeping tablets bad for me? Because they're working, but if you think...'

'I personally think you should consider them a temporary measure. It's great that they're working for you and helping you sleep, but probably not a permanent solution. What does your doctor think?'

'He's happy to prescribe more whenever I need them, but you know, I don't want to have to rely on them forever, I suppose. Maybe I'll try something else just to see if it helps.'

She ended up choosing the PTSD counselling and with the help of my supervisor, we referred her to an expert in that field. I also secured a discount for her. I was told it was because it was my first referral, but I think my empathetic supervisor may have pulled a few strings.

Over the following weeks I saw the rest of the family members, some coping better than others. I agreed to a follow-up session with Callum's sister, as she seemed to be struggling more than the others. I started to get more and more bookings, and my schedule for two days a week was already full. It looked as though I may have to fit clients in on my alternative Wednesday off and maybe even one or two evenings after school.

Mae's son, Dr Seán, was referring clients to me and Amy was advertising my services all over town, including the library where her mum had worked. I realised I'd have enough work-experience hours built up to apply for my independent licence soon.

It was proving difficult to give my teaching

career the time and energy it required. I discussed the demands of my new clinic with Maureen. She understood that if business continued in this upward trajectory for me, there would be a high possibility that I wouldn't return to Sacred Heart in September. She'd known this was coming for a while and had mixed feelings about it. On the one hand, she didn't want to lose me, yet she could plainly see how enthused I was about my practice. It reminded her of me when I'd first started teaching—full of hope, positivity and love for my profession.

And that was exactly how I felt now about Triple D.

*   *   *

Oddly enough, I never felt lonely in the house by myself. Teaching and Triple D consumed most of my time and I talked with Amy pretty much every day. Her positive energy and lust for life reminded me so much of Patricia. And it truly felt like my sister was still around, rooting for me every step of the way.

On Sunday afternoons when my paperwork was complete, I'd sit on my patchwork chair by the window and reflect on the week that had gone by. I'd smile to myself, acknowledging the little successes, and purse my lips when reminded of the work that still needed to be done. Sometimes I'd ring or text someone to check in, but on this particular afternoon I was feeling lazy and a little introspective after a busy week.

I got up to get my notebook to jot down my next day's to-do list. But there were no pages left so I opened the drawer to find a new one. That was when I spotted Phil's CD—the one he'd gifted me in London. *Why hadn't I listened to it yet?*

Maybe I'd been worried it would stir up his image in my mind and distract me from all I had to do. Surely, on hearing his song recommendation, I'd well up and be reminded of how much I missed him. While those were valid reasons, I also had another, more practical one—no CD player. Wasn't all music invisible now? Phil was showing his age by giving me an old-fashioned gift like this. But when I pictured his apartment in my mind, I remembered that he was a sentimental old fool when it came to collecting DVD's and CD's.

I desperately wanted to listen to it, especially now that I'd literally just come across it at the back of the drawer. I decided to send out a message on the Neighbourhood Watch Whatsapp group to check if anyone had a CD player I could borrow. To my surprise, I got a reply straight away. Old Mr Foster down the road had one and said he'd send it over pronto.

I fetched a brandy before carefully removing the CD from its wrapping paper and peeling off the plastic film. When the ancient stereo was delivered by Mr Foster's son, I very quickly forgot about my to-do list.

I thought I might hear an angelic voice like

that of Conor O'Brien from Villagers that Phil had once played for me, but instead, a rasping, gravelly voice boomed from the player. The initial clapping and sounds of the jazzy music perked me up instantly. I turned it up so I could hear every word. Tom Waits introduced each song before he sang. And everything he said made me smile.

I was immediately transported to a jazz club in LA and felt surrounded by an upbeat, expectant crowd hanging on his every word. I was a nighthawk in the diner! I paused the music, dashed to the kitchen to top up my brandy and ran back to listen to the rest.

As I sat on my patchwork chair by the window listening to 'Intro To Better Off Without A Wife' and belly-laughing hysterically, I realised that singledom in one's fifties was vastly underrated.

This song would warrant a text to Phil later on. This whole album was so Phil. He wasn't mine and maybe never would be. There was every chance he'd fall into someone else's arms in Sydney and I knew that was a looming possibility. But there was no escape from the fact that we shared a special connection for which I would always be grateful.

I listened again to my favourite track before picking up the phone to invite Amy and the kids over for dinner. I sank back into my chair and for some reason thought of the people I'd loved and lost throughout my life. I felt blessed, content, and at peace as I wiped away tears, while simultaneously trying to contain my inner smile.

Epilogue

I read a book written by a well-known Irish psychologist who said midlife begins at fifty. I hoped that was true, because that meant I was only halfway through.

My work at the clinic not only consumed me, but enlightened me with each new client that walked through the door. I felt validated when they took my advice and tried strategies I'd recommended.

But, without doubt, my biggest success story was when Callum's mum, Jean, informed me that the PTSD counselling was so beneficial to her that she'd decided to train as a counsellor herself. Having gone through the pain of losing a loved one to suicide she felt she had the experience to help others.

This knowledge also helped me in my healing journey. I booked in with Jean as soon as she qualified, not only to support her, but also to relieve myself from the remnants of grief and regret that occasionally plagued my dreams. Who better to share my hurt with than Callum's mother, who also happened to have had a fleeting friendship with Patricia? It was cathartic to confide in someone who so naturally understood.

For my fifty-second birthday, I went out on a whim and booked a trip to Mexico. I could almost hear Patricia laughing in her grave as I secured my ticket. I extended an open invitation to everyone I considered a friend. I hadn't a clue if anyone would be mad enough to join me, but I didn't care. I'd go alone anyway with confidence—there was no stopping me now!

I felt like this was the beginning of a whole new chapter in my life. I finally felt strong enough in my fifties to cultivate the life I truly desired. And if experience had taught me anything, it was the wisdom to know that this kind of freedom is rare...and should never, ever be underrated.

The End

NOTE FROM THE AUTHOR

Many thanks for reading my book. If you enjoyed it, I'd be very grateful if you would leave a review. As an independent author, reviews help so much to inform potential readers.

If you'd like to connect, you can reach me at rachelraffertybooks@gmail.com

And I reveal juicy gossip about my characters, hidden scenes and stories of my writing life in Ireland right here: rachelrafferty.com/diary

Printed in Great Britain
by Amazon